Pascal Garnier

Pascal Garnier was born in Paris in 1949. The prize-winning author of more than sixty books, he remains a leading figure in contemporary French literature, in the tradition of Georges Simenon. He died in 2010.

Emily Boyce

Emily Boyce is in-house translator at Gallic Books. She lives in London. She has previously translated *The Islanders*.

Too Close to the Edge

Too Close to the Edge

Pascal Garnier

Translated from the French by Emily Boyce

Gallic Books

London

A Gallic Book

Original title : *Trop près du bord* © Zulma, 2010

English translation copyright © Gallic Books 2016
First published in Great Britain in 2016 by
Gallic Books, 59 Ebury Street, London, SW1W 0NZ

A CIP record for this book is available from the British Library
ISBN 978-1-910477-25-0

Typeset in Fournier MT by Gallic Books
Printed in the UK by CPI (CR0 4YY)
2 4 6 8 10 9 7 5 3 1

To Nathalie

Papa, papa...
Serge Gainsbourg

As the peeled potato fell into the pan of water, it made a loud *plop* which rebounded off the kitchen walls like a tennis ball. Holding the peeler still in her hand, Éliette paused to savour the moment; this – she was certain – was pure happiness.

Buffeted and battered by a year of uncontainable sobs, her heart had at last steadied itself like the green bubble in a spirit level. There was no particular reason for this new-found calm, or rather, there were a thousand: it was May, the rain was beating against the windows, there was baroque music playing on France Musique; she was making her first vegetable jardinière of the season (fresh peas, lettuce hearts, carrots, potatoes, turnips, spring onions, and not forgetting the lardons!); the Colette biography she had picked up the day before at Meysse library was propped open at page 48 on the living-room table; she wasn't expecting anyone, and no one was expecting her.

All these little things along with countless others meant that for the first time since Charles's death she did not feel lonely in the house by herself, but one and indivisible.

The France Musique presenter introduced the next programme in a voice which called to mind a priest with a pickled liver. Éliette opened her eyes and set to work on the last potato, challenging herself to peel it in one continuous length. Then she cut the carrots and turnips into perfectly evenly sized pieces, gave the lettuce a shake and plunged her hands into the colander of peas with a sigh of pleasure. The sensation of the little green marbles rolling between her fingers was as enjoyable now as it had been in childhood, when she helped Mémé Alice shell peas. It was the reward for her hard work.

Her grandmother's kitchen was like a women-only hammam. The windows were clouded by aromatic steam. Mémé Alice's gnarled arthritic fingers resembled moving tree roots as they sliced vegetables, trussed chickens and kneaded dough as soft and white as the flesh of her arms. There was no talking in Alice's kitchen, only singing. Edged with a thick layer of grey fluff, her upper lip quivered as she hummed 'Les Roses blanches', 'La Butte rouge' or 'Mon vieux Pataud'.

With her sizeable girth straining against the front pocket of a huge black apron, Mémé Alice strongly resembled the cast-iron stove which seemed to blaze constantly. Indeed, such was the affinity between the two that you almost wondered in whose belly her dishes had been baked, stewed or roasted as she brought them to the table, huffing and puffing like an old steam engine.

Despite the fact she now had three grandchildren of her own, Éliette would never be a Mémé Alice. The children called her Mamie – probably because she was not old or fat enough to be a Mémé, her hair not long enough to pin up in a taut bun like a cartoon elderly aunt. These days, old age was regarded as an insult, an ugly omen from which children should be shielded. It brought to mind visions of prolapse, support stockings and many other repulsive things besides, as hideous a prospect as death itself. Éliette was sixty-four.

She was one of those people who had always been and would remain attractive in a wholesome, obvious sort of way. She had never needed to give nature a helping hand. Just a touch of lipstick now and then when she and Charles went out of an evening, purely for the raspberry-flavoured kisses. Even the few wrinkles gathered around her eyes brought a new charm to her face. It was as though time had polished her with beeswax. Only Charles's passing had slightly dulled the sparkle in her eyes, and placed her smile in permanent parentheses.

The two of them had shared forty years of untarnished love before Charles was suddenly carried off by cancer two months before he was due to retire. They had already started packing for their move from the Parisian suburbs to this house in the Ardèche, where life was supposed to be a never-ending holiday.

They had bought the former silk farm thirty years earlier. Year after year, they had spent every spare moment doing it up to turn it into the haven of peace that sadly she alone now enjoyed. After Charles's death, Sylvie and Marc had tried to put her off going through with the move.

'It's madness, Maman. What are you going to do with yourself, stuck down there in the back of beyond? It's a nice place to go on holiday, but living there full-time is another story.'

'But I won't be on my own. The Jauberts are here!'

'The Jauberts! I mean, they're decent people and every-thing, but all they do is go on about tractors and frosts and their disappointing onion crop. And as far as neighbours go, that would be your lot. You haven't even got a driving licence and the nearest village is eight kilometres away. How are you going to do your shopping? On a bike?'

'Why not?'

'And what if you're ill?'

'I've got a telephone.'

'It's ridiculous, completely ridiculous!'

For a few months Éliette had been undecided, kicking about the flat in Boulogne with nothing on the horizon but the TV schedule and the possibility of a Sunday visit from her children and grandchildren. Then one day …

'I'm selling Boulogne and moving to Saint-Vincent.'

Marc rolled his eyes and Sylvie, as usual, burst into floods of tears. Of course it was madness, but that was exactly what she was missing: a touch of madness to stop herself sinking into reason.

She moved house in late spring. For the first few months, Éliette quelled her doubts by indulging in an ever increasing range of activities, some more productive than others: she repainted doors and shutters that didn't really need doing; planted vegetables and flowers, most of which died of boredom before they had even budded; set out to learn Italian on a tape recorder she never quite worked out how to use; spent considerable sums on subscriptions to lifestyle magazines – Grow Your Own Veg, Sew Your Own Curtains,

Learn to Love Yourself, and so on; and started a diary, but never got beyond the first three pages. Then autumn came along.

Until this point, Marc and Sylvie had taken turns helping out with her screwball schemes, but they had their own lives, families and jobs to get back to, and at the beginning of September they both returned to Paris, leaving their mother in the care of the Jauberts, who lived on a farm two kilometres away.

Rose and Paul Jaubert were slightly younger than Éliette, but looked a good ten years older. Although on the face of it they did not have a great deal in common, thirty years as good neighbours had forged a true friendship which Charles's death and Éliette's permanent move to the silk farm had taken to a new level. The Jauberts now saw themselves as Éliette's protectors, an arrangement as well meaning as it was burdensome.

Almost every evening until late November, Éliette was obliged to join them at their Formica-topped kitchen table for a supper washed down with generous helpings of whatever happened to be on TV. It was almost impossible to wriggle out of these nightly invitations without causing offence. She eventually did so on the pretext of needing time alone to collect her thoughts, an excuse the Jauberts accepted without understanding, but which must have come as a relief to them as much as to her.

Thus Éliette had won the freedom not to watch TV but to listen to the radio, read or, most often, lie in bed for hours on end, stiff as a corpse, willing sleep to hurry up and come.

At times like this, the Mogadon pills always had the last word. Not that she was complaining: there is nothing worse than having to share your solitude with other people. In any case, she still saw the Jauberts almost every day, especially Rose.

'Here, I brought you some soup, a bit of salad, some onions and courgettes. I'm going shopping; do you need anything?'

Éliette's fridge was constantly filled with vegetables that regularly ended up on the compost heap. No, she didn't need anything, or if she did, that would be the one time Rose stayed away. This was how the idea of a microcar came about. She had spotted a few of them on the winding roads near her home and envied the septuagenarian couples calmly crawling along at a snail's pace, unfazed by the honking horns and flashing headlights of furious motorists on the verge of shunting them into the ditch.

'For crying out loud! Those things should be banned! Honestly, I could go faster in my tractor!'

Éliette held her tongue while she and Paul overtook one on the way back from the market, but secretly she could picture herself at the wheel of one of those smart little motorised buggies. She thought about it during the day and dreamed of it at night, like a child longing for a big toy for Christmas. It took all her skills of persuasion to convince Paul to take her to a dealer.

'Éliette, why don't you just take your driving test? Then you could buy a real car. My cousin's selling his Renault 5, in perfect condition.'

'No, I'd be bound to fail.'

'But Rose took hers at forty-five!'

'Well, I'm sixty-four. And anyway

'But Éliette, it's not a car; it's a toy, at that!'

'Exactly, it's a toy I'm after.'

Thanks to Charles's pension and the sale of could easily afford to indulge her whim. Paul reluctantly agreed to drive her to Montélimar, where she purchased a magnificent top-of-the-range cream Aixam. It took a little while to get used to driving it up the dirt track that led to her house, but after a few days she was able to go backwards and forwards, left and right without too much damage to the bumpers. Her first solo expedition (a round trip of about twenty kilometres) gave her as much of a thrill as if she had piloted a plane. Window down, hair blowing in the wind, she sang at the top of her lungs: '*Je n'ai besoin de personne en Harley Davidson …*'

The vehicle had changed her life. To begin with, Rose had seemed put out, as if Éliette had taken a lover. But in the end everyone got used to the idea, and even laughed about it.

'Ah, there goes Éliette in her bubble car!'

Yet Madame de Bize was hardly in the first flush of youth. The lines on her face, hollowed by constant smiling, heralded the impending onset of her forties; her fulsome hips, whose immodest curves had once been celebrated by friends of both sexes, were becoming heavy …

She was interrupted in her reading of the Colette biography by the sharp ring of the telephone. It was midday, so it could only be Sylvie. This was her regular slot. She called once a

.rom the office, just before going for lunch.

'Hello, Maman? It's Sylvie.'

'Hi, darling. How are you?'

'I'm all right, just knackered. Justine's got measles.'

'Poor little thing!'

'What's the betting she's going to pass it on to Antoine?'

'You did the same to me, you and your brother. Do you think you'll make it down for Whitsun?'

'Oh, yes. She'll be better by then.'

'Are you still planning to arrive on Friday?'

'That's the idea. Anyway, how are you?'

'Fine. I've just made myself my first vegetable jardinière of the season.'

'You lucky thing! Richard and the kids don't like veg. I'm jealous!'

'I'll make you one when you're here.'

'With lardons and crème fraîche?'

'Of course. And how are things with Richard's job?'

'Oh, you know what the property market's like at the moment ... He's got a few things in the pipeline. He's been travelling a lot. Are you sure you're OK?'

'Absolutely! It's been stormy the last couple of days, but it's supposed to cheer up in time for the weekend. I'm reading Colette's biography and very much enjoying it. What about you? What are you reading?'

'Oh, I don't have time to read. When I'm not working or looking after the kids, doing the shopping ...'

'I know, darling. We ought to retire when we're young and work when we're old.'

'You work all your life and then look what happened to Papa! Sorry, Maman. I'm just so stressed at the moment. I can't wait to see you and have some home comforts.'

'Don't you worry. I'll look after you and you can put your feet up. What about your brother? I haven't heard from him. Have you arranged things with him?'

'Oh, I never know what's going on with Marc. He always has all the time in the world. Everything's always hunky-dory. I've no idea how he does it. Actually, I do know: it's Sandra who does everything – the kid, the house – always with that vacant smile on her face. The perfect housewife!'

'Don't be unkind about your sister-in-law. She's very nice.'

'Very, and I think that's what annoys me most about her. She never lets that mask of domestic bliss slip. It's easy when you don't have a job.'

'That's not fair. Sandra's very ... traditional. Your brother earns a good living; she likes looking after the house. What's wrong with that?'

'You're right, yes. She's very traditional. Anyway, let's talk about something else. No issues with your little car?'

'None at all. It works like a dream!'

'Maman ... are you happy?'

'Of course I am, sweetheart!'

'I don't understand how you do it, living in the middle of nowhere. How does anyone manage to be happy in this lousy world? You know, just the other day ...'

Éliette was no longer listening. She loved her daughter, of course, but at this precise moment she could not care less

17

about the little one's measles, or Richard's problems at work, or what Sylvie thought of her brother or sister-in-law or this lousy world.

'Sorry to interrupt you, darling, but I can smell something burning in the kitchen.'

'Oh, OK. We can talk about it another time. I'll call you if there's a problem, but we should be there on Friday evening.'

'Bye, love.'

Nothing was burning in the kitchen. There was just the reassuring *blub-blub* of the jardinière simmering gently on the stove. Éliette pushed back a log which had slipped in the grate. The smouldering embers glowed like the ruby-red seeds of a ripe pomegranate. It was not cold, but the rain and the pleasure of reading by the hearth had given her the urge to light a fire. She returned to the sofa and let out a sigh.

Confinement breeds confinement. Though her isolation might at first have felt limiting, she soon realised she had no choice but to accept it, settle into it, even become comfortable with it, to the extent that the world beyond her four walls seemed like nothing but chores. Of course she loved her children and her children's children just as she might love the sky, the trees, the mountains, life in general – but after two days in their company she could no longer stand the sight of them. It was probably exactly the same for them. Eight hundred kilometres was a long way to travel to see her for Whitsun, even without counting the cost of the journey. There was a degree of obligation on both sides, but if the family had not come, she would no doubt have missed them. It was paradoxical, but that was the way it was. It had taken her a while to admit it to herself: she needed them, but after twenty-four hours couldn't wait for them to leave.

Tonight it would be Marc's turn to call and tell her which day he would be arriving, and tomorrow he would call again and say he would probably be later than expected, what with work … She would grumble a little for the sake of form, but the truth was she didn't give two hoots.

All the minor irritations that had irked her for years now left her totally indifferent. What did it matter if there were nine people or five for dinner? She could always make an omelette, a salad … The only thing that now differentiated her children from anyone else was the pang of emotion in her chest when they said goodbye. After all, what is a child but a kite you fly and then let go, for it to reappear among the clouds? She had read somewhere that we were all the children of children.

The jardinière was divine. As she munched her way through it, she felt like a rabbit grazing a veg patch. The nap that followed was equally delectable. By the time she woke up, the rain had stopped. A baby-blue sky extended as far as the eye could see. There was a smell of washing powder in the air, of sheets drying on the breeze. In the garden the bay leaves were fringed with water, each droplet holding a ray of sunshine within it. All around, the mountains were steaming, streaked ochre and purple and foaming minty green to freshen the wind's breath.

She asked herself if it might be an idea to undertake a commando mission to the supermarket in Montélimar today, rather than await the inevitable trolley gridlock at the end of the week. Without much deliberation, she told herself it would not. Her solitary way of life had made her overly wary of approaching a town of more than eighty inhabitants. But there was nothing in her fridge or cupboards that two couples and their children might want to eat after a long journey. One way or another she would have to make the trip, today or tomorrow.

It was only four o'clock, and it was no longer raining. Éliette decided to grin and bear it and went up to her room to change. She was ashamed at the sight of herself in the mirror of her wardrobe: shapeless woollen cardigan, baggy-kneed leggings, thick socks and grubby clogs. This was what country life looked like: a far cry from a Fragonard shepherdess frolicking on a swing in a flouncy dress. While nature was blossoming in a riot of colours and scents, she was slowly turning into a hideous caricature of the frumpiest pages of the La Redoute catalogue. While she had never been a slave to fashion, Éliette had always made an effort with her appearance. But with nobody to look nice for …

'You're letting yourself go, old girl. Take a look at yourself: you're like something off the compost heap!'

Earlier in the week, Rose had been extolling the benefits of the disgusting nylon overalls she wore day in, day out. 'They're just so practical! You wash them and half an hour later they're dry again. And even if you put a bit of weight on, they're so roomy!'

If her body had not rebelled in the face of such an outrage, Éliette could almost have been convinced. Stripped down to her bra and knickers, she began emptying her wardrobe in search of something decent to wear, holding various dresses, jumpers and blouses against her body, but all she saw reflected in the mirror was the sad face of a glove puppet poking out from behind a curtain. Tears welled in her eyes. One last shirt fell to the floor to join the pile of sloughed-off skins, each more tired and outdated than the last.

She cupped her breasts, turned sideways on and posed like a toreador, fluffing up her hair. Her chest was still firm, her stomach flat. Plenty of women half her age would envy a figure like hers. But what use was it to her, with no one around to touch it? Her body had become as pathetic as a bouquet of flowers left to wilt on a station platform by a jilted lover.

Even Rose, bulging out of her vile overalls like a saucisson d'Arles, was a thousand times more alluring than she was. Paul was a red-blooded man; they probably did 'it' every night … How long had it been since Éliette had made love? Since the beginning of Charles's illness. What was the point in still being slim and attractive and faithful to the memory of a man reduced to a stinking pile of bones at the bottom of a pit? What had she been trying to prove since becoming a widow? That it was possible to survive without sex? Who was she trying to fool?

A few weeks earlier, Paul had helped her put up a curtain pole in her bedroom. She had been standing on the stepladder hanging the curtain when her foot had slipped. Paul caught her by the waist and gently lowered her to the floor. For a few seconds, his hands had remained on her hips and their eyes had locked bizarrely. She could not help but feel a little unsettled when she recalled that moment, as she had done several times.

It was like a fist inside her belly. Cursing that fat cow Rose and the rude health of her husband under her breath, she pulled on a black jumper, black trousers and a pair of flats the same colour.

Putting aside the storms of the last two days, spring had come remarkably early this year. Even at the beginning of the month, summer had been in the air. Éliette had rarely found nature so sensual: the merest blade of grass seemed swollen with sap, leaves undulated on the breeze, and every shrub appeared to quiver with a frenzy of animals mating in its midst, setting Éliette's senses firing. She was buzzing all the way to the supermarket, and on her arrival went straight to the freezer section. She kept her head down, convinced that every man in the shop was staring at her.

In the vegetable aisle, she blushed as it dawned on her she had filled her trolley with courgettes, aubergines, carrots, cucumbers and even an enormous long white turnip weighing nearly 300 grams, which she struggled to make herself see in a culinary light. It was stronger than she was; a kind of inflammation of her mind was slowly turning the supermarket into a sex shop. She found herself getting drunk on the potent cocktail of shame and desire. Having finished her food shopping, she was drawn to the clothing section where she picked up the sexiest underwear set Continent could offer, along with a pair of skinny jeans and two low-cut tops that even the boldest fashionistas in Montélimar would have deemed too risqué to wear.

As she unloaded her trolley, she avoided the gaze of the

woman on the checkout, pulling her blonde hair over her forehead so that no one would see the word SEX branded across it. She stumbled weak-kneed out of the shop as if emerging from an orgy, piled the shameful evidence of her countless vices into the back of the microcar, and breathlessly set off home.

'You're totally loopy, you poor old thing! Totally loopy!'

She had never driven this fast before. She couldn't wait to get home, put all this food away in the fridge and find a home in the bottom of a cupboard for these clothes she would never wear.

So she had suffered a bit of an 'episode'; there was no need to make a drama out of it. She would laugh to herself about it later while finishing the leftover jardinière, having taken a Mogadon to overcome the ache in the small of her back, strangely pleasant though it was. She came off the main road at Meysse and took the little road along the River Lavezon. The river water was the colour of milky coffee. The poplars were bowing dangerously low and the sky was puffing out cheeks newly refilled with soot. In ten minutes the storm would break. She had just crossed the little bridge when the Aixam swerved, made a curious fart noise, zigzagged across the road and ended up on the verge.

'Shit! Shit! Double shit!'

It had never crossed her mind that she might get a puncture. Yet that was exactly what had happened to her front left wheel, barely two kilometres from home. Panicking, she got out and circled the vehicle, giving the tyres little kicks as mechanics do when trying to diagnose a problem. All this achieved was to make the little car quiver on the spot like a stubborn ass refusing to walk on. The first raindrop fell on her forehead as she was calling the heavens to come to her aid. The manual she retrieved from the glove compartment, hitherto untouched, was incomprehensible double-Dutch covered in pictures which bore no relation to anything she could recognise. Yes, she knew the jack and the spare wheel came into it somehow, but they were so well hidden!

It didn't occur to her to run back to the house, call Paul and ask him to give her a hand. Instead she contemplated suicide, for example by throwing herself into the muddy waters of the Lavezon. It was at that moment she saw him coming. A man, but not from round here. A man in a three-piece suit, jacket slung over his shoulder, briefcase in hand. A man who seemed to have come a long way judging by his heavy, steady gait and the hair slicked to his forehead. It was like a scene out of a Western: beneath a low sky, a stranger walks calmly towards his widescreen destiny.

'Problem?'

'I've got a flat … I don't know how to use … all this.'

The smile he shot her opened a hole inside her head.

'Mind if I take a look?'

He appeared to be in his forties, not very tall, not especially thickset, with a baby face. His shoes and trouser bottoms were covered in mud. As he set to work on the wheel, the rain began to drop like a portcullis. Éliette could not tear her eyes from his muscular back, which showed through his sodden shirt. He was finished in under ten minutes.

'There you go. Done.'

Standing face-to-face, streaming with water like two freshly landed fish, they burst out laughing. The sky no longer existed.

'Thanks. Can I give you a lift somewhere?'

'That would be great. I broke down myself, a few kilometres away. I was trying to find a phone.'

'I live just up the road. Hop in, quick.'

The windscreen wipers struggled to give some definition to the muted watercolour landscape. The Aixam skidded as it climbed the muddy track. Back at the house, after several trips back and forth to unload the boot, they stood breathless in the kitchen, droplets of water fringing their eyelashes.

'I'll get some towels. Goodness me, I need wringing out!'

They towelled their hair dry and took in the sight of one another: all fluffy and dishevelled, like chicks emerging from their shells. They cracked up again. Outside, thunder was rolling above the roof.

'Would you like some tea?'

'Please.'

Éliette was cack-handed, or all fingers and thumbs: she couldn't think where the cups lived, almost tipped over the kettle and banged into a chair while vainly trying to think of something witty to say.

'It's been pouring down like this for two solid days! It's because the last month has been so hot.'

'Probably.'

The water was taking an eternity to come to the boil.

Everything was too slow, and yet she would have liked this moment to go on and on. Every now and then she threw a glance at the man sitting at the table, discovering him bit by bit as though piecing together a puzzle: the nervous long-fingered hands, the blue vein pulsating in his neck, the blond cowlick on his forehead, the brown eyes that seemed to be searching for something on the ceiling ...

'Are you from round here?'

'No ... I'm from Paris.'

... nice mouth, but bad teeth ...

'So your car broke down too?'

'Um ... yes. Must be something in the air today.'

... a deep voice which hesitated over every word, as if they all started with a capital letter. A little boy in a man's body, two opposites inhabiting the same skin. The kettle began to whistle.

'Here we are. It's ready!'

They drank their tea without saying a word. The patter of the rain filled the silence. From time to time their eyes met, they smiled shyly at one another and looked away.

'Nice place you've got here.'

'Yes, I like it. But it took an awful lot of time and effort to do it up. When we bought it, thirty years ago, it was a wreck. We were living in Paris at the time, in Boulogne. All our holidays were spent cementing, plastering ... We wanted to retire here. Sadly my husband died two years ago.'

'I'm sorry.'

'I decided to come and live here on my own. I have pictures of what it used to look like—'

Before Éliette could finish her sentence, the phone rang.

'Excuse me.'

'Of course.'

Why oh why had she ever had children? It could only be Marc. She went into the living room and answered the phone with irritation in her voice.

'Yes? Oh, it's you, Paul ... Yes, no. What's going on? ... What? ... Patrick! ... Oh, Paul, I'm so sorry ... and Rose? ... Of course ... of course ... I'll come right now, Paul ... Yes, see you very soon.'

Éliette returned to the kitchen, ashen.

The man noticed and instinctively rose from his chair.

'Bad news?'

'That was my neighbours. Their son has just been killed in a car accident ... I have to go round.'

'Of course. I'll go ...'

'No, don't. It's still raining and the next village is eight kilometres away. The phone's in the living room and there's a phone book underneath it. But I doubt you'll get anyone to come out at this time. Anyway, make yourself at home. There's wood by the fire if you want to dry off.'

'That's very kind of you ... I don't know what to say ...'

'What about "See you later"?'

'See you later.'

The truth was that beyond feeling sorry for Rose and Paul, Éliette was not especially upset to hear Patrick had died. She had never liked the kid. Even as a little boy he had been a nasty piece of work. Sylvie and Marc had hated him because he was always throwing stones at dogs, cats, chickens, people in general and especially his brother, despite being the younger by four years. Serge, unlike Patrick, was the very model of sweetness and sensitivity. He had left the farm as soon as he could and was now a teacher living somewhere near Grenoble. His family seldom saw him. It was Patrick who was the apple of his parents' eyes, despite the fact he openly despised them. But he was a good-looking lad with the gift of the gab, and had just passed his exams at the agricultural college in Pradel with flying colours. He would one day inherit the farm, since his brother wanted nothing to do with it.

Old Bob pulled half-heartedly at his chain and bared time-worn canines as Éliette parked outside the house. Paul opened the door to her. He had the face of a zombie, his eyes were red, and the breath from his wet mouth was thick with pastis.

'Ah, Éliette, Éliette …'

For the first time in the history of their friendship, he put his arms around her. He smelt of the sweat of misfortune. She felt as if she were falling from the ladder again, only this time he was the one leaning on her, and that changed everything. It took a little effort to extricate herself from the embrace.

'It's awful, awful … We don't understand …'

'Oh, Paul. You poor thing … Where's Rose?'

'In the kitchen. I didn't know what to do. I'm sorry for dragging you out in this weather.'

'Please, don't mention it. What are friends for, after all?'

Éliette had apologised to everyone when Charles died too. People are always ashamed of the misery that has befallen them, as though it were an act of divine retribution for a long-forgotten sin of theirs. Walking unsteadily, Paul led her into the kitchen where Rose seemed to be dozing, rocking back and forth in her chair near the stove. When Éliette put her arms around her, Rose turned to show a face wrecked by tears, washed of all expression. Her flabby skin fell in folds, as trickles of wax on a candle stump.

'It's not even as if he was coming back from a knees-up! … He wasn't even drunk! … In broad daylight!'

'You let those tears out, Rosie. It'll do you good. I know how you feel, you know …'

'I know you do.'

'I brought you something to take. Have this and put yourself to bed. Tomorrow, things will be a bit clearer. There's nothing else you can do.'

'Yes. We need to look after Paul. He's in pieces …'

'Of course. Don't you worry.'

Paul sat slumped, shoulders hunched, elbows on the Formica table top, a bottle of pastis in front of him, despite the fact he usually barely touched the stuff. Éliette filled a glass with water from the tap and handed Rose a tablet.

'I'll take her up to bed and I'll be right back down, OK, Paul? Paul?'

'Huh? Yes, yes.'

Rose let herself be guided up to the bedroom, which was decorated in the most ghastly brown and orange flowery wallpaper. The blue satin quilt gave a kind of sigh when Rose fell onto it. A piece of boxwood fell off the crucifix above her head and went spinning onto the carpet.

'He did whatever he wanted. He came top in everything ... It's not fair, no, not fair ... Have to look after Paul. We're old ... We've become old all of a sudden.'

'Don't worry, I'm here. You need to sleep.'

'I'll never sleep again.'

'You will. Just let yourself go.'

In the mirrored wardrobe door, Éliette could see herself holding Rose's hand. Her neighbour's face was hidden behind her round belly; in the foreground was one bare foot and another with an old slipper hanging off the toes. The scene was dimly lit from above. This was where they made love, where the couple's children had been conceived ... The wedding photo on the bedside table seemed to come from another age, from a time when children died not in car accidents but in wars, or crushed between the jaws of some agricultural machine.

Rose was extremely house-proud. There was not a speck of dust or the merest cobweb to be seen, whereas Éliette collected them like the works of old masters. How did they have sex? From the front? From behind? It was ridiculous, but it was all she could think about. She tried to rid herself of these visions of copulation – all the more obscene in the circumstances – to bat them away like persistent flies. She felt Rose's hand go limp. She was asleep, mouth open and nostrils pinched. Éliette wriggled her hand free and tiptoed out of the room.

Paul had not moved an inch. He seemed to have become permanently embedded in the table edge and was staring straight ahead.

'She's asleep. It'll do her good. You should do the same, Paul.'

'Huh? Yes, yes.'

Éliette smelt something burning. The remains of a stew were turning to charcoal on the hob. She turned the heat off under the pan and came to sit across the table from Paul.

'How did it happen? Do you want to talk about it?'

'Happened around midday, the gendarmes say. They found him at two o'clock down the bottom of a ravine off the little road at Le Coiron – you know the one. Nice views but it's so narrow and wiggly. Someone had left a car parked on the road, right before a bend. Maybe Patrick was going too fast, but what was that driver thinking, leaving his motor in a place like that? The road's tight enough as it is! Even if he'd run out of petrol, even on a hill ... I don't know ... You'd push it or something, you'd get it off the road! He was trying to get round it ... He died instantly ... When we heard, I tried to call you, but you weren't in.'

32

'No, I was out shopping in Montélimar. Have you told Serge?'

'Yes, he'll be here tomorrow. What do we do now?'

'There's nothing you can do except go to bed and sleep next to Rose. She mustn't be left alone. You need to look after one another. All these dark thoughts going round in your head, they're not getting you anywhere.'

'You're right, of course ... You know, the strange thing is, the guy never came back for his car. The gendarmes called me earlier. They think it was stolen.'

'That is odd, yes.'

'Yes ... and what are all these kids doing, driving around like mad things? Five this year, just in our little patch! Last one was young Arlette, Robin the builder's daughter, remember? In November?'

'Yes, I remember.'

'They think they're untouchable! How many times did I tell him, "Patrick, you're better off getting there late than not getting there at all"? Might as well have been talking to a brick wall! He stopped listening to me a long time ago. Thought other people were a waste of space, his father especially. I gave that kid everything ... Would you like a bite to eat, Éliette? I've warmed up some leftover stew.'

'No, thank you. I've got someone waiting for me at home.'

'Oh, I didn't know. I ...'

'It's fine. Besides, I think your stew's burnt. I just took it off the heat. Can't you smell it?'

'No. Another time, then?'

'Of course. Do you want one of the pills I gave Rose?'

'No, thanks. I've got that.'

He indicated the half-empty bottle of pastis with his chin.

'Take care of yourself, Paul. It's no use letting yourself go. Remember you've got Rose to think of.'

'It's kind of you to have come, Éliette. At times like this you need your friends.'

'I was glad to help. You did the same for me when Charles died. And tomorrow, Serge will be here.'

'Yes ... but it's not the same with Serge, we don't speak the same language. Patrick and me, we were salt of the earth. We didn't need to chat ... I love Serge just as much ... only, I never feel totally comfortable around him.'

'He's just very different from his brother, that's all. I'm heading off now, Paul, so you should go to bed. If you need anything at all, just call. Either way, I'll pop in tomorrow morning.'

He nodded, but was no longer listening. His gaze was clouding over, his eyes turning the colour of pastis. Éliette patted his shoulder and left the kitchen.

Outside, the smell of thoroughly burnt food lingered in her nose and throat. The rain had stopped and a single star was twinkling above hills as rounded as Paul's back. Old Bob barely turned his head as Éliette passed him. The look in his eyes expressed something beyond weariness. Éliette started the car, and once the lemon-yellow light of the Jauberts' window had disappeared from her rear-view mirror, she broke into sobs. It wasn't only the Jauberts she was crying for, but Old Bob, the single star, the dark hills and herself. The tears flowed on and on like the swollen Lavezon river, washing away all her sadness. Paul and Rose were neither friends nor family, more like fellow passengers on an overnight train. They had nothing in common besides existing in the same space and time.

She had once read a definition of poetry as 'two words meeting for the first time'. There was an element of that in her relationship with her neighbours. It was so easy to love like-minded people, but when chance threw someone totally different in your path ... like the man awaiting her at home, whose name she didn't even know. What if he had gone? He might well have called a taxi. Éliette lifted her foot off the accelerator. The truth was she had spent the whole time at the Jauberts' thinking of him. That was probably why she had forced Rose to go to sleep and encouraged Paul to do the same. She had to some extent been trying to get shot of their sadness. And why not? Today was not just any day! Her heart was pounding in her chest as she put her foot back on the pedal. What if he had got hold of a mechanic? What if ...? She saw the light at the living-room window and let out a cry of joy. For the first time in so long, someone was waiting for her.

He was sitting by the hearth where a fire was blazing. He straightened up when Éliette came in, as though caught doing something he shouldn't.

'You didn't get through to a garage then?'

'Er ... no.'

'I'm not surprised – we're out in the sticks here. At least the rain's stopped. It's clearing up.'

'How are your friends?'

'He was their favourite son. I gave them some sleeping pills. Nothing else we can do. Such a terrible blow. But it happens all the time round here; people drive like lunatics; they're a law unto themselves. Every weekend, they roll out of the discos and it's carnage on the roads ... Listen, here's what I think you should do. It's too late to find a garage or hotel round here. I have plenty of spare rooms. Why don't you spend the night here and I'll take you to a garage tomorrow?'

'That's very kind of you, but you don't know me ...'

'Well then, introduce yourself!'

'Étienne Doilet.'

'Éliette Vélard. So, what do you say?'

'Well ... yes.'

'I'll warn you now: if you're a murderer, I have very little to lose, and there's nothing here worth stealing unless you count the walls. Are you hungry?'

'I think so.'

Éliette warmed up the leftover jardinière, cracked four eggs into a frying pan and opened a bottle of wine. The fluctuations of the weather served once again to fill the awkward silences. But after two glasses of wine, Éliette's tongue loosened and she began lauding the region to Étienne, who was a first-time visitor here.

'You know, the Le Coiron road – it's on my mind because that's where my neighbours' son had his accident – well, it's magnificent! The landscape changes every couple of kilometres. On the plateau, you're right up in the mountains. It's glorious. Oh, by the way, there was a funny thing about Patrick's accident: someone had left their car in the middle of the road. Patrick was trying to get round it when he plunged into the ravine. And no one ever came back for the car. The gendarmes say it was stolen. Strange, isn't it?'

'Yes.'

'Well, anyway. Oh, I'll tell you another wonderful road: the one from Saint-Thomé to Gras. It follows the river and ... is something wrong?'

Étienne was making a strange face, as if he had just bitten into a lemon.

'No, no. I'm fine!'

'I'm boring you, playing the tour guide. I don't get out much!'

'Not at all, honestly. It's nice to hear someone talking so passionately about where they live.'

'Thank you. Hang on, where was it that you broke down?'

'Me? Um ... This is ridiculous, but I have to tell you the truth. I didn't break down.'

'Oh!'

'It's so stupid ... OK, I was in the car with my girlfriend and we had an argument. Things got heated; I told her to let me out and she did. Leaving me in the middle of nowhere ... Not clever, I know.'

Éliette burst out laughing. Étienne's cheeks were red and he hung his head like a little boy owning up to doing something silly.

'I'm sorry, Étienne. It's a nervous thing.'

'Don't apologise. It was such a childish thing to do, but I couldn't help it. I've never been in a situation like that before.'

'There's no need to be embarrassed about it. It's quite funny, really!'

'Can I smoke?'

'Go ahead.'

Smoking was not normally allowed at Éliette's house. Marc was asked to go and puff on his cigarette outside, and even then only on condition no butts were dropped in the garden. But this evening she was enjoying watching the smoke emerging from Étienne's nostrils like the genie from Aladdin's lamp.

'Where's the dog?'

'What dog?'

'It says "Beware of the dog" on the front door.'

'It's a deterrent; we've never had dogs. If anyone came to the door late in the evening, I'd shout, "Charles, keep hold of the dog!" ... It makes me feel safer. But no one ever does come. That's why I don't need a real dog.'

'Don't you get bored here?'

'You must be joking! I've no chance to be bored. Only today I've had a flat tyre, a death at the neighbours' and a stranger in my house! And it's like this every day!'

Étienne stubbed out his cigarette. When she smiled, Éliette looked like a teenager.

'Oh, I almost forgot: your son, Marc, called. I think he was a bit taken aback when I answered. I told him you were at your neighbours' ... He'll call again tomorrow.'

Marc's phone call brought Éliette back to a reality she would have preferred not to have to face that evening.

'Yes. I have a son and a daughter and three grandchildren. I'm a grandmother.'

'That's nice.'

'Why?'

'I don't know ... You have a family ... You're not on your own.'

'No, I'm not ... Goodness! It's almost midnight! I ought to have been in bed at least two hours ago. I'll show you your room.'

Out of the bedrooms Éliette offered him, Étienne chose Sylvie's. Whitewashed walls, film posters, amateur photos of twisted tree trunks and overexposed sunsets, an old teddy bear at the foot of the bed, a bunch of dried flowers in a stoneware pot, a few children's books, teen magazines, the odd splash of pink.

'If you get cold, there are extra blankets in the wardrobe.'

'Thanks. I think I'll sleep well.'

'Good. Right, then ... Good night.'

'Good night, Éliette.'

There's a man in my house, just the other side of that wall, in Sylvie's room. I can hear him coughing, getting undressed, slipping between the sheets. I don't feel like going to sleep; I won't take a Mogadon. I want to play it all back in my head, see him appearing at the bend in the little bridge, changing my tyre, driving home with me in the rain ... Then later, when I got home from the Jauberts' and found him waiting for me beside the hearth. Someone was waiting for me tonight, Charles ... I told him about us; maybe I should have said more about you ... He's not asleep; I can hear him turning in bed, see the light under his door ... I'm alive, Charles, I'm alive.

Éliette's nostrils quivered at the wafts of toast and fresh coffee. She opened first one eye and then the other, and sat bolt upright. *He's up already?* Yawning, she let her head fall back onto the pillow and stretched out as if trying to touch the walls either side of the bed. The alarm clock showed eight thirty. Slippers, dressing gown, despairing glance in the mirror.

Étienne was at the sink finishing last night's washing up. The draining rack was sagging under a typically masculine pyramid of precariously balanced plates, glasses, cups and saucers.

'Morning.'

'Morning, Éliette. Sleep well?'

'Very well. You should have left all that; I'd have sorted it out later.'

'It's no trouble. I like washing up in the morning. It helps me clear my head. People shouldn't complain so much about household chores. I've made coffee, but maybe you'd prefer something else?'

'I'm more of a tea drinker, but it's fine. It's good to ring the changes.'

'I can make tea! I'll put the kettle on.'

'OK then.'

Éliette sat on a chair, hands dangling between her thighs.

The sun filtering through the part-closed shutters cast a ladder of light on the wall. It was strange to have had the role of hostess taken from her. He had robbed her of her little morning habits. She missed the radio and felt vaguely awkward, as if she were in a hotel.

'I'm not used to being waited on.'

'It's not as bad as all that, you'll see. What do you use to strain your tea?'

'There's an infuser in the left-hand drawer.'

Steam rose from the tea and twirled around the piercing ray of sunlight reflected off the glazed surface of the bowls.

'Not easy finding your way around a new kitchen. I hope I haven't made too much of a mess of things.'

'No. Just the bowls. These ones are for soup.'

'I do apologise!'

'I suppose I can live with it, just this once.'

'Madame is too kind!'

They laughed. Étienne unfolded the napkin he had wrapped around the toast to keep it warm. For once, life seemed not to need an instruction manual.

'It'll be warm today. Look how the light's flooding in.'

'It's like being on holiday. We could have had breakfast outside ...'

'Let's do it!'

They sat and finished their bowls of tea on the enormous stone slab that served as the front step. The sun flowed into them like honey trickling deep into their bones. Eyes half closed, Éliette pointed out the features of her garden. It was surrounded by a dry-stone wall, surpassed in height only by a fig tree and a cypress. To the right, an old barn housed a long table and benches.

'That's my summer dining room. We've had some good times in there: barbecues in the evening with candles in glass holders, the children ... I have a telescope. On summer nights you can see the stars up close ...'

'It makes me think of houses in Morocco, the internal courtyards. They smelt of jasmine, incense burning on the embers, fresh mint tea ... The drumbeats ... as if marking their rhythms on the taut skin of the moon. The stars twinkled, and the sound was like the copper jingles of a tambourine.'

'Are you a poet?'

'No, I'm just remembering.'

'Do you know Morocco well?'

'I was there for a while.'

'For work?'

'In a sense. Would you like another cup of tea?'

'No, thank you. I'll go and have a shower. Are you ... in a rush? I mean, for me to take you to Montélimar?'

'No, no. Take your time. I'm fine right here ...'

'In that case I'll leave you to your memories.'

Where would the world be without soap? Éliette sang as the water gushed out of the shower head onto her newly confident body. Étienne was clearly in no hurry to be leaving. It was lovely, what he had said about Morocco. What was he doing over there? And here? ... Perhaps they could get the barbecue out? ... He looked tired: why not suggest he stick around for a couple of days? The children were not coming until the weekend ... It could be a digression, a short aside in the long monologue her life had become.

Plans were building to a lather in her head and the toothpaste was foaming in her mouth when she heard shouts coming from the garden. She ran to the window. A taxi had parked outside the front door. A girl in her early twenties with a messy heap of dyed red hair, in black sunglasses, a T-shirt and ripped jeans, was marching towards Étienne, swinging her bag above her head. Before Étienne could scramble to his feet, the bag hit him full in the face, knocking him backwards.

'Fucking idiot! What have you done, you bastard?'

The bag struck Étienne a second time on his back as he tried to get up, holding his arms in front of him for protection. Blood was pouring from his eyebrow.

'Agnès! Stop it, for fuck's sake! Something in there weighs a ton!'

Éliette raced outside, wet-haired, toothbrush in hand.

'Whash going on out here? Have you losht your mind?'

'Who's this?'

'The owner of thish house.' (Éliette spat out her toothpaste.) 'I must ask you to calm down. As long as you're on my property, you'll sort out your quarrels with your boyfriend in a civilised manner!'

'My boyfriend? Please! He's my father, my fucking father!'

Open-mouthed, Éliette looked first at Étienne, who was holding both hands to his brow, and then at the girl, who was kicking at every piece of gravel and raising clouds of dust. Meanwhile, the taxi driver had heard all the shouting and got out of his car. Éliette knew him. He had taken her to Montélimar several times before she got her microcar.

'Is there a problem here, Madame Vélard?'

'No, it's fine. Just a family squabble.'

'All right then. Either way, this little madam needs to pay my fare. I've got other jobs to get to.'

The girl took a note out of her bag and handed it to the driver without a word or a glance in his direction.

'Your bags?'

'Leave them by the door.'

The driver shrugged, waved goodbye to Éliette and drove off. The courtyard was filled with the chirping of crickets, accompanied by cymbal crashes of sunlight.

Éliette leant over Étienne. 'Does it hurt?'

'It's OK. I'm sorry ...'

'I'll get a cold compress.'

The girl had sat down on the stone outside the door and lit a cigarette. Éliette almost had to climb over her to get inside the house. She heard Étienne mutter, 'Jesus, what the hell have you got in that bag?'

'My camera. Sorry. I hope it's not fucked ...'

While she searched the medicine cabinet for a dressing and antiseptic, Éliette heard them arguing in low voices on the doorstep. A name kept coming up, spoken by the girl with a note of panic: Théo. Who was this kid who had just parachuted into the middle of Éliette's dream? How had she got here? And why? So many unanswered questions colliding inside her head. The telephone rang out like a clarion call. As she passed the front door, she dropped off Étienne's dressing and ran back into the living room.

'Hello, Maman?'

'Yes, hello, Marc.'

'What's the matter? You're out of breath.'

'I was in the shower.'

'Oh, sorry. Do you want me to call back?'

'No, it's fine.'

'Who was the guy who answered the phone to me last night?'

'A friend. I was at the Jauberts'. Oh, Marc, I have to tell you something. Patrick was killed in a car crash yesterday. That's why I was at their house.'

'Patrick? ... Jesus!'

'It's hit them hard. I can't talk for long, I told them I'd pop round this morning. Serge is on his way.'

'Yes, I understand ...'

'Are you still coming on Friday?'

'That's the plan, yes.'

'OK, well, I'd better go, son. See you soon! Love you.'

Her hand was still on the receiver when the phone started ringing again.

'Madame Vélard, it's Serge ... Jaubert.'

'Hello, Serge, dear. How are your parents?'

'Not great. Maman would like to see you.'

'Of course. I was about to come round. I'll be there in ten minutes.'

'Thanks. See you soon.'

Éliette bounded up the stairs, threw on the clothes she had been wearing the day before, and hurtled back down again. Something akin to the blades of a food processor was mincing up her slightest thought. She was incapable of forming complete sentences, telling herself only: keys, glasses, bag ... Stepping from the gloom inside the house to the full sun of the garden was like walking into a shower of flames. For a few moments she saw nothing. Étienne and his daughter seemed to have disappeared. Then, shielding her eyes with her hand, she caught sight of them curled up like two cats in the darkness of her 'summer dining room'. They were leaning on the long wooden table and smoking silently, one's gaze concealed by dark glasses, the other's obscured by a thick bandage over his left eye.

'Better now? You've calmed down? Show me ... That's an impressive black eye you're going to have there!'

'What about this one? Impressive enough for you?' The girl lowered her glasses. Her right eye was a magnificent green, but the left was ringed bright purple.

'Étienne, did you ...?'

'No, he didn't, but it's *because of* him.'

'Agnès, please!'

'Look, I don't want to know. Let's just say it gives you a family resemblance. All I ask is that you avoid making a scene while you're under my roof. I have to go round to my neighbours'. You know the situation, Étienne. Things are bad enough as they are. Can I trust you?'

'Absolutely, Éliette. I really am sorry. It was a misunderstanding.'

'All right. See you later then.'

The one saving grace of the morning's dramas from Éliette's point of view was to have discovered that Agnès was Étienne's daughter and not his girlfriend, as she had first thought. The rest was as confusing as it was unsettling. In what kind of family did a daughter whack her father round the head with a camera while hurling abuse at him? She had been equally shocked by Étienne's completely passive response. Why had he phoned Agnès? After all, that was the only possible explanation: he had called her last night while Éliette was with the Jauberts ... And that bruise on Agnès's face: *It's because of him* ... Something was telling her to send the two of them packing, but the memory of the pleasure of Étienne's company the previous day put her off. She would wait and see. For now, she was coming up the Jauberts' drive as Serge came out to greet her, another young man of similar age hovering behind him. Both had very short hair and moustaches. Serge looked utterly crushed.

'Hello, Madame Vélard.'

'Come on, call me Éliette.'

'Yes, sorry. This is all so ... This is my friend Zep. He's German but he speaks very good French.'

'Pleased to meet you. So, how's your mother?'

'Still a bit woozy after those drugs you gave her, but ...'

'And your father?'

'He hasn't said a word. He's like a plank of wood.'

48

The three of them entered the house. It was cool inside and the smell of coffee vainly tried to cover that of aniseed. Paul hadn't budged from the position he had occupied the day before, sitting with both elbows on the table. Only the empty pastis bottle testified to the passage of time. Rose lifted her puffy face, broke into sobs and rushed over to throw herself on Éliette.

'My boy! My little boy!'

'There, there, Rose. I'm here ...'

Serge turned his watery eyes to the window and squeezed his friend's hand. Éliette noticed the gesture but made little of it, turning her attention back to Rose, who no longer even had the strength to cry.

'Come with me, Rose. Let's go outside and get some fresh air while we talk. It'll do you good. You too, Paul. You can't stay sitting at that table for ever. You've got to keep going.'

Serge leant towards his father to help him up. Without moving, Paul said under his breath, 'Don't you touch me.'

Serge held out his hand.

'Papa ...'

'I said don't put your dirty queer hands on me!'

The slap aimed at his son met empty space. Carried by the momentum, Paul toppled over and fell onto the tiled floor. Rose was open-mouthed, frozen but for her chest which rose in quick shallow breaths, as if hiccuping. Serge and Zep knelt down beside the father.

'He's fine, he's snoring. He's pissed out of his head. Let's put him to bed.'

Éliette and Rose watched the two boys lift Paul's body and haul it up the stairs.

'Come on, Rose. Let's have a walk; it'll calm us down.'

'Yes ... Why did Paul say that?'

'Say what?'

'"Your dirty queer hands".'

'He's had too much to drink; he doesn't know what he's saying. Come on – show me how your geraniums are getting on.'

Agnès emerged from the kitchen carrying a bottle of pastis, a jug of water and two glasses on a tray.

'Agnès, you're going too far.'

'Why? She's cool, she won't mind. Anyway, I feel like a drink. If we weren't in the shit, I could imagine we were on holiday. OK, so when Théo's contact gave you the package, you got straight back on the train to Paris?'

'Yeah. But I'd been mulling it over since the day before. Six months back, when I finished my time in Morocco, I had so many good intentions. But you have no idea how hard it is to get used to life on the outside. I'm gonna be forty-five ...'

'But you'd have made ten thousand for a return train journey!'

'What the fuck did I care about ten thousand when I had that whole package under my seat! I kept thinking about Théo's face when he chucked me the five thousand upfront. Small change. All my life I've had nothing but small change from guys like Théo. You reach a point you can't take any more. The train stopped at Montélimar, and I got off.'

'You're crazy, my poor papa.'

'Don't call me Papa. It's ridiculous.'

'OK. So then what? How did you end up here?'

'I panicked a bit once I was on the platform. Everything was going too fast. I couldn't hang around; I stood out like a sore thumb. I went into the car park and stole a car. Once I got behind the wheel, I calmed down. I headed out of town on back roads without much idea where I was going. I stopped in the middle of nowhere to stretch my legs and think things over. But I didn't regret it for a second! I found a little green meadow with clumps of white flowers. I lay on my back and watched the clouds drift past. It made me think of summer camp. I was eight years old in Le Chambon-sur-Lignon, one of the few good times in my life. The weather was always fine, even when it rained. It smelt clean; we were always hungry. We built tree houses. I thought to myself: if there's one safe place for the two of us in this shitty world, then that's it. I was picturing a little chalet in the forest, you coming to join me there ...'

'I'd have preferred the Caribbean.'

'I got back in the car and drove along this incredible little road that wound up the mountain ... Just my luck, I ran out of petrol halfway up. Couldn't leave the thing there, so I got out, started pushing and ... this guy comes roaring round the bend. It was so fast, I didn't see it happen. I just heard the screech of brakes, the crack of broken branches, the crunch of metal, and then nothing. I ran down into the ravine. The guy was dead. He was young ... What was I supposed to do? ... I went back up to the car, wiped everything down, the steering wheel, the seat, the door ... My head was on fire: anyone could turn up at any minute ... I grabbed the briefcase and legged it through the woods.'

'No way! You just dumped everything?'

'Yeah. Afterwards I walked for ages through fields and woods ... It was getting dark when I met Éliette. She'd broken down. You know the rest.'

'You're a magnet for trouble, aren't you?'

'Want to know the best part?'

'What?'

'The neighbours' son, the one who's just been killed in a car crash ...'

'Yeah? ... No! You mean he's ...'

'I'm almost certain. She was telling me how the accident happened last night.'

'Now that's the icing on the cake! Do excuse me, I think I'll serve myself another!'

Father and daughter locked eyes for a moment and burst out laughing. They were still in fits when Éliette's Aixam came bouncing up the dirt track.

'Looks like everyone's in a better mood. Have you made up?'

'Yes, Éliette, everything's fine. I hope you'll forgive us for the scene we made.'

'Let's put it behind us. I could do with a drink myself, actually.'

'I'll go. I'll fetch some ice as well.'

As Agnès was getting up, Éliette settled herself on the bench opposite Étienne. She closed her eyes for a second and a firework display went off inside her head, images flying around like meteors: Paul sitting at the kitchen table, Étienne changing the wheel, Rose's slipper in the mirror, Serge squeezing Zep's hand, Agnès hitting her father with her bag, Étienne doing the washing up ...

'It's all a bit much, isn't it?'

'It is, rather. I'd been moaning that my life had become a bit monotonous of late. I can't complain about that any more!'

'Things have been a bit crazy for me lately too. I'd like the whole merry-go-round to stop. But we won't be under your feet for too long. Agnès lives in Lyons. I called her last night to come and get me. Unfortunately she had a little scrape in the car, hence the black eye and terrible mood. She was halfway here when it happened, so she had to get a train and then a taxi.'

'So long as there are no more fisticuffs in my garden, you're no trouble at all. In fact I don't know how I'd feel about being on my own at the moment.'

Agnès brought cold water and ice cubes.

'Y'know, Éliette – is it all right if I call you Éliette?'

'Yes.'

'There's a barbecue there, and sausages in the fridge. Do you think we could ...?'

'Agnès! You're overstepping the mark.'

'No, she's right.'

'Great! I'll sort it. I love making a fire!'

All tension disappeared once the barbecue was lit. They laughed easily and talked about everything and nothing, making the most of this momentary bright spell in the knowledge it was a temporary reprieve. Corroded by a sort of rust as they may have been, Agnès's twenty years added a spark to the conversation. Éliette watched in wonder. Agnès was nothing like she or even her daughter had been at twenty. She was both more mature and more carefree. She occasionally used a word or expression that Éliette didn't understand and Étienne would step in to translate for her. Éliette found Agnès's relationship with her father fascinating. Sylvie would never have spoken so freely to Charles, even though they were considered an open family. Some of the dubious situations father and daughter talked about planted a seed of doubt in her mind as to the true nature of their relationship to one another. And yet she found nothing distasteful about their stories, to the extent that she too began sharing things she had not told anyone in years. She was swooping into an unknown world and landing gently – aided, no doubt, by the nice cool rosé. And why not? There were so many other worlds ... Paul and Rose's, Serge and Zep's, Sylvie's, Marc's ... an infinite galaxy that could never be explored in a lifetime. It was as good as closing her eyes while being whirled around on a carousel.

'Are you all right, Éliette?'

'Yes. But I'm going to have a shower and get changed. I'm too hot in these clothes.'

Once Éliette had left the table, Agnès lay down on Étienne's side of the bench and rested her head on his thigh.

'What now?'

'Haven't got a clue. As long as we're here, nothing's going to happen. Are you sure you weren't followed?'

'Yes. Théo came round before you called. He could knock me around all he liked, I didn't know anything. Then you rang. I got the student across the hall to bring my bags down – you know, the one who's got a thing for me. I told him to take a taxi and wait for me at Gare de Lyon. I strolled out of the building a quarter of an hour later and took the métro.'

'I told Éliette you lived in Lyons, to explain why you're here. I said I called you last night to ask you to pick me up. Only, you had an accident somewhere between Vienne and Valence, which is how you got your shiner. Later on you need to pretend to call the garage where your car is, and then tell us it won't be ready until Thursday. As far as I can make out, her kids don't get here until Friday. That gives us two days' grace.'

'Right. Only trouble is I've never set foot in Lyons. Not that that makes much difference. Have you got cash?'

'A thousand, tops. Plus the briefcase.'

'Your two kilos of coke aren't worth shit around here. Who are you going to sell it to – the goats? The yokels?'

'I know! But we'll find a solution. We just need time to think. I need to stop for breath.'

'Poor Papa, you really know how to land yourself in the shit. To think I didn't even know you existed a month ago!'

'Please, can we not talk about that?'

'But it's not your fault! Stop with the guilt. How were you to know the girl you were about to cop off with was your daughter? Everyone calls me Lol at Théo's place, and I was only a year old when you left. If you hadn't found the photo of Maman, you'd still be none the wiser. I might have got pregnant and given birth to a hideous monster! Bleurghhh!'

'Please, Agnès. It's not funny.'

'Fine! Whatever. So, this coke, have you tried it?'

'No.'

'Well, you should.'

'Now don't start poking your nose ...'

'Hang on a minute! You don't know how to be cool. The only person who can find you a buyer is me. So I want to know what it is I'm selling, OK? And I'll also need a sample. You don't just deal two kilos like that.'

'OK. The briefcase is upstairs, in the room I slept in. But just a sample!'

Birds were dabbling in the blue sky, the air hummed with the chirping of crickets, and plant smells mingled with wisps of smoke from the dying embers of the barbecue. Étienne was wondering what it would take to become a Trappist monk. Faith? Couldn't be that difficult. He had believed in a lot of things in his time, so why not a little guy nailed to a wooden cross? The truth was that freedom had never done him any good. Being locked up for the last few years had given him more of a taste for being inside than out. That was what he liked about this walled garden. We can only truly escape from within.

He would never have got mixed up in a crazy scheme like this if he hadn't found Agnès again. How had he landed up at Théo's place? ... Through a friend of a friend of a friend, most likely. Since getting out of prison, he had been knocking about around Paris. There was a big crowd that evening.

The mirrors were covered in trails of powder. Tequila, beer, spliffs, wild Parisian nights. He didn't find it fun any more. He was there because he had to be somewhere after all. The girl with red hair had got up from Théo's lap and come to sit next to him.

'You look as bored shitless as I am.'

'Yep.'

'Shall we get out of here?'

'And go where?'

'Your place!'

'I'm in a hotel. Not a good one.'

'I don't give a shit.'

They made love all night and they did it well, very tenderly, pausing now and again for a line of coke or a drink. It was the first good thing to happen to him in months. He slept for the whole of the next day and she came back in the evening. They had dinner together at a little place near the hotel in the eighteenth arrondissement, and they picked up where they had left off the night before. It was like a fairy tale for little kids. In the morning, on his way to have a piss, he had used Lol's bag to shoot up. Among the objects that fell out of it were a photo of a woman he had known all too well and an identity card in the name of Agnès Doilet. He couldn't help letting out a cry, at which point the girl turned over in bed and opened one eye.

'What's going on?'

Étienne threw the identity card and photo onto the bed.

'What about it?'

'I'm your father, Agnès! I'm your father!'

Éliette had decided to be bold, and she did not regret it. The jeans and T-shirt she had bought the day before made her look ten years younger. She smiled blissfully into the mirror as though touched by a fairy's wand. On her own, she would never have taken these clothes out of their packaging. As a little girl, whenever she was given something new to wear, she would find an excuse to go straight out and show it off. But that was back on the busy streets of Paris ... What was the point in doing the same here? Today, though, she had an audience in the form of Étienne, and Agnès, whom she bumped into as she went from her bedroom into the corridor.

'Oh, Éliette, I wanted to ask: you don't have a set of kitchen scales, do you?'

'Kitchen scales?'

'Yes, I have some letters to post and I need to weigh them.'

'Um ... yes, I must do. Have a look on top of the kitchen cupboards.'

'Thanks. Ooh, love the T-shirt. The colour's great on you.'

Étienne had got out two sunloungers. He was stretched out on one of them with his head in the shade and his feet in the sun. He appeared to be asleep. Éliette sat down beside him. The heat trapped inside the garden walls made the air hum. She closed her eyes and every sound and smell became magnified. It was like dissolving in a kind of bouillon.

'Your house is lovely. It's like you.'

'I thought you were asleep.'

'No. I'm having such a good time, I don't want to miss a thing.'

'Are you ... are you thinking of leaving soon?'

'Agnès needs to call the garage to see when her car will be ready. Could be this evening.'

'I know we've only just met, but ... it's really nice having the two of you here.'

'The feeling's mutual, I think. An unexpected interlude, for all of us.'

'It's funny. Nothing happens for months and then it all comes in an avalanche!'

'It's like hunting. You spend more time lying in wait than you do shooting.'

'In two hours, we'll have known one another for twenty-four hours.'

'Long enough to have shared memories: the tyre, the storm, your neighbours' son's passing, Agnès's grand entrance this morning, a barbecue, your metamorphosis from widow in black to butterfly in blue. The colour really suits you.'

'Why didn't you tell me you had a daughter?'

'You didn't ask.'

'True. Come to think of it, I know nothing about you.'

'That's about all there is to know.'

Agnès appeared in the doorway. Her feet were bare and she was wearing a micro miniskirt and a men's shirt with barely a button done up.

'I've put the scales back, Éliette. I made a phone call as well; you'll have to let me know what I owe you. It was about my car.'

'Don't mention it.'

'It won't be ready until Thursday. Nightmare!'

Éliette could barely contain a sigh of relief. Agnès came to sit on the ground between the other two. She was sniffling, like a red-haired poodle.

'Do you have a cold?'

'It doesn't take much – a shower, a bit of a breeze and that's it! So, Étienne. What shall we do?'

'Éliette, would we be outstaying our welcome if ...?'

'Not at all. As I said, my children don't arrive until Friday, so it's no problem.'

'Thank you, Éliette. But we'll take care of the shopping and cooking. Agreed?'

'Agreed. We can sort that out tomorrow. We've got everything we need for tonight. Oh, looks like we've got a visitor ...'

The police van parked in front of the gate. Two gendarmes got out. They were red-faced, with rings of sweat under the arms of their shirts. Éliette went to greet them.

'Bonjour, Messieurs.'

'Bonjour, Madame Vélard ... Monsieur, Mademoiselle.'

Étienne and Agnès barely nodded.

'Have you come from the Jauberts'?'

'Yes. What a tragedy. No matter how many times you see these things happen, it's still a shock. And it makes you wonder what gets into these kids the minute they have a steering wheel in their hands. Twice we'd arrested Patrick! ... Though it's a bit different this time. Anyway, since we were just down the road and we know you like riding about in your little car on the back roads, we wondered if by any chance you might have come across anybody on foot who might have seemed a bit ... strange?'

'No. I went to Montélimar yesterday and then ...'

As she replayed the previous day's events, she instinctively turned to Étienne before going on.

'... and then I came home again. I didn't notice anything strange.'

'Just asking on the off-chance. And Monsieur, Madame, you didn't see anything either?'

'We arrived on the train this morning.'

Étienne's reply rolled straight off the tongue, as if he had learnt the line by heart. Éliette was somewhat taken aback.

'Well then ... We won't keep you.'

'Is it to do with the other car?'

'Yes, Madame Vélard. We've identified the owner. His vehicle was stolen around midday yesterday from the car park at Montélimar station. The fuel tank was empty. The thief must have panicked. Stupid. Right, we're off. Goodbye, Madame Vélard, Monsieur, Madame.'

Even after they had gone, a blue stain seemed to linger where they had stood. Étienne lay with his arm across his face and his head thrown back. Agnès was rolling pebbles through her fingers and Éliette was desperately trying to find the key to escape the heavy silence. The light was tinted copper and the house's stonework was blushing pink. Agnès got up suddenly.

'I'm going to do the washing up. I need to move.'

She disappeared, swallowed up in the shadows of the doorway.

'Éliette, why didn't you tell the gendarmes how we met?'

'Because ... because it's beside the point! You had an argument with your girlfriend and she left you in the middle of nowhere, isn't that right?'

'Yes, of course.'

'And the reason you told them you'd arrived on the train this morning was to avoid having to go into details like that.'

'Exactly. Why complicate things?'

'In the past, I always had to be in control, to understand and check everything. I couldn't feel at ease without answers and solutions. But since Charles died, I've tended to let things come and go as they please.'

'Did you love your husband very much?'

'Yes. The way we felt about one another was never in doubt. But ... how can I put it? It's as if that was another life. I think of it now as if it belonged to someone else. I've changed. I don't know if the life I had with him would suit me nowadays.'

Éliette got to her feet and began pulling up a few weeds around a scrawny rose bush. Étienne watched her through half-closed eyes. She was like a ripe fruit whose sugar was turning to honey. Certain people, like certain plants, flowered several times in one season. Others would never bear a single fruit: no sooner had they blossomed than they were already wilting. Étienne thought of himself as akin to an avocado stone: you kept its bottom wet in a mustard jar and it sprouted one measly stem, busting its guts to produce a single flower as pathetic as a flag at half mast. So much must come down to the soil the plant was grown in, the amount of water and sun it got. Above all, it rested on the great gardener on high knowing what he was doing ...

'You've got green fingers then?'

'Let's just say I try.'

'Unlike me; I've managed to kill fake flowers before.'

'That's quite a feat!'

'I know. I'm quite proud of myself.'

Through the open kitchen window they could hear Agnès singing Gainsbourg: *'Inceste de citron, papa, papa ...'*

Agnès's sniffle did not appear to have cleared up, but strangely it had given her a burst of boundless energy. She had done the cooking and laid the table; now she was like a moth fluttering around the flickering light of the candles. All that was left of the daylight was a trace of purple at the bottom of the sky, with the rolling mountains starkly outlined against it. As at lunchtime, the conversation covered all kinds of topics, but everyone made a conscious effort to avoid talking about themselves. Hiding behind tales of other people's adventures was like swanning about at a masked ball. They had already polished off two bottles of rosé and Étienne was opening a third when a headlight swept like a brushstroke over the line of poplars at the entrance to the drive.

'That must be Serge and his friend. I rang earlier to see how they were. I told them to pop in for a drink, depending on how things were at home.'

The two young men appeared, their pale clothes almost phosphorescent against the dark mouth of the garden gate. Éliette did the introductions. Agnès made yet another excuse to slip inside the house, this time in order to fetch glasses. Éliette noticed that these comings and goings seemed to be getting on Étienne's nerves. Serge's face was drawn; Zep never took his eyes off him.

'So, how is everything?'

'Not great. Things are OK with Maman, but Papa's not speaking to me. My uncle and aunt came down from Aubenas this afternoon. They're staying a few days. I took the opportunity to get on with some of the formalities, going to the undertakers' and so on. Any excuse to get out of the house. The funeral's on Friday.'

'OK. I'll go and see them tomorrow. Try not to blame your father. He's having a hard time. It might not look like it, but he's more fragile than your mother.'

'I don't blame him. It just hurts, that's all. You saw how he was this morning when I tried to help him …'

'He was drunk.'

'It's almost worse when he's sober. It's as if he thinks I'm the one who killed Patrick. I'm hurting too, even though Patrick and I didn't get on. I saw him two months ago in Grenoble; he wanted me to sign something. We had a row. You don't know at the time you're never going to see someone again; it's only afterwards …'

Serge had tears in his eyes. Zep placed a hand on his shoulder. Étienne stood up, uncomfortable, made his excuses and went into the house.

Agnès was sitting on the bed tidying away her little kit: mirror, straw, razor blade.

'Don't you think you've had enough tonight?'

'This is the last one! You're so fucking tight! God, it's good though. What's your problem?'

'Nothing. I'm sick of hearing about that accident.'

'Chill out. Nothing's gonna happen. And anyway, Éliette

has the hots for you, big time. I wouldn't mind having her as a stepmother. By the way, where am I sleeping tonight?'

'Don't know, don't care.'

'Thanks very much! OK, I'll stop pissing around. I think I've got an idea, a client.'

'Who's that then?'

'A guy who works in the movies. I've sold to him before; there's never been a problem.'

'Nothing to do with Théo?'

'No, different network. Only thing is, if we want to get rid of the whole lot at once, we can't be too greedy.'

'And where is this guy?'

'Down on the Côte d'Azur at the moment, I think. I'd have to make a phone call.'

'I don't know … We don't want to rush things.'

'Rush things?! Do you have any idea of the shit you've got us into in the last twenty-four hours? D'you really think we have a choice? We're not on our holidays at Auntie Éliette's, dearest Daddykins. We've got two days at most before we need to get the hell out of here, as far away as we can get, because let me tell you, Théo's not going to let two kilos of good coke go without a fight, especially not to you. Don't forget you already pinched his woman – that would be me!'

'He didn't give a shit about you. That's why he gave the job to me!'

'How stupid are you? Do you really think you'd have got it if I hadn't made him give it to you?'

'You promised me you wouldn't see him again!'

'Oh, calm down … You didn't have two coins to rub together … Anyway, don't worry, nothing happened. So what do you think?'

Agnès was right. They had to make a move, try something. There was no use pretending, and yet …

The sound of Éliette's voice calling from the garden made him jump. He leant out of the window.

'Étienne, when you come down, would you mind bringing the telescope with you? It's in my room, next to the wardrobe.'

'Yes, yes, of course.'

'There's a magnificent sky tonight and Zep's a bit of an astronomer!'

'Righty-ho. On my way.'

How dumb the stars looked, as dull as the streetlights lining the motorway. Agnès was lying on her back, knees bent, thighs bared, smoking a cigarette. The white triangle of her knickers was curved like a scallop shell.

'Well?'

'OK. But be careful.'

Agnès joined the other four in the garden a quarter of an hour later. They were drinking wine and staring up at the stars. Zep was pointing up at the sky, reeling off clever-sounding names that his accent made sound even more exotic. They took turns pressing their eye to the telescope and exclaiming, 'What a view!' All except Étienne, who passed on his go, preferring to keep a suitable distance between himself and the stars looking down on him in scorn.

'I prefer the bit in between, the darkness. The part you can't see.'

They all stopped talking after that. They let space seep inside them; the sky was reflected on earth. Serge and Zep had their arms round each other's necks; Agnès was lying on the grass, arms outstretched, Éliette on one of the loungers with her hands behind her head; and Étienne sat perched on the bench, chin in his hands, elbows on his knees. There was no movement, only a twinkling like an aura around each of them. They had become a kind of constellation, in a scenario brought about by what we call chance, for want of a better word. It lasted for a split second, or an hour … Serge and Zep whispered a few words in each other's ears and stood up.

'Éliette, it's getting late. We should head back up there.'

'Up there? Oh, yes! Come back whenever you want.'

'Thanks, Éliette. It's so nice to be able to … just be ourselves. Good night. Good night, Étienne. Lovely to meet you. Good night, Agnès.'

The three left behind watched the other two dissolving into the night, the same way they had come. Agnès stretched her limbs.

'Mmm! It's so pretty. You can see angels all over the place tonight … Éliette, where am I sleeping?'

'Wherever you want, love. The room next to your father's.'

'It's love, now, is it?'

'Oh, sorry, I …'

'It's fine. Love is all around. Good night!'

*

Neither Éliette nor Étienne knew how to take their leave. Perhaps they did not wish to. They both watched the light come on at Agnès's window. Earlier, Zep had explained to them how stars were dying and being born all the time. The sky was sparkling. The light bulb in the bedroom went out, but its image stayed imprinted on their retinas for a long time afterwards. All his life, Étienne had been in bars at closing time, among the last ones standing at the end of the party. He liked being around people who refused to accept it was over, who fought a losing battle against the inevitable.

'Éliette, how about a game of "Say what you're thinking"?'

'How does it work?'

'You don't think about it. You just say the first thing that comes into your head.'

'OK. Do we take it in turns?'

'Yes.'

'Right then. Say what you're thinking.'

'I'm thinking it's too soon for everything.'

'I'm thinking we ought to get several lives.'

'I'm thinking my death will serve no purpose and that's a missed opportunity on God's part.'

'I'm thinking I don't want to make up my mind whether I'm too hot or too cold.'

'I'm thinking my family has a lot of dirty linen to air and it's getting out of hand.'

'I'm not thinking about my family, but I've got a big pile of dirty linen too.'

'I'm thinking that if I hadn't had a daughter, I wouldn't necessarily have had a dog.'

'I'm thinking we don't have to do anything, but everything is important.'

'I'm thinking no one is ever happy and that's our only source of satisfaction.'

'I'm thinking everyone else is better than me.'

'I'm thinking we shouldn't want to please everyone.'

'I'm thinking everyone else lies except me, and it's not a nice thought.'

'I'm thinking of all the times a lie has helped me to tell an unexpected truth.'

'I'm thinking of a quote of De Gaulle's: "I've spent a lot of time pretending, and usually it has worked."'

'I'm thinking we should have been warned the world was ending.'

'I'm thinking I'm dreading the sun rising in a few hours.'

'I'm thinking tomorrow is not another day.'

'I'm thinking by going too far you get back to where you started.'

Their fingers had become entwined; it wasn't a game any more.

Éliette had not taken in a word of the news, despite the fact the radio was droning in her ear. They could have told her the world had ended and still she would have carried on sipping her tea, staring into space, lost in thought. A fly was keeping her company, buzzing from one jar of jam to another, totally absorbed in its essential function: eating and washing its sticky feet in the tiny pool of tea beside the teapot. Éliette felt in perfect harmony with the fly. The minimalism of its existence suited her down to the ground. To aspire to more than eating jam and washing one's feet in tea seemed unnecessary. It had pretty eyes as well, this fly, and wings for which Éliette would have gladly swapped her feet. Agnès wafted into the kitchen wearing only her large men's shirt. She mumbled a hello as she sailed past without a glance in Éliette's direction. She sat down and poured herself a tea with such delicacy that she chipped the cup.

'Morning, Agnès. Sleep all right?'

'No. It's too quiet here; it keeps me awake. What about you two?'

'I slept very well. As for Étienne, you'll have to ask him yourself. I think he slept on the sofa in the living room. I heard snoring.'

'Oh!'

With her mass of wild red hair and big black eye she looked like a clown who had messed up his act.

'Shall I do you some toast?'

'Er …. OK.'

'It's always like this the first few nights when city people come to stay. The silence gets to them. But they get used to it.'

'You need time for that.'

'For what?'

'To get used to it. I've never had time to get used to anything. Just as well – I don't like habits. Why did he sleep in the lounge?'

'I don't know. He was still in the garden when I went up to bed. He was asleep on one of the loungers.'

'Pissed?'

'No, just tired, I think. Here's your toast.'

'Thanks. He's always tired. Some people have dogs for companions; he's got his tiredness. I'm heading off today; I'll be back tomorrow night.'

'Oh! OK then.'

'I can't stay in one place. Gotta keep moving. I've got mates on the Côte. I'll visit them and then head back up.'

'Right, well, if you like ...'

'Can we borrow the limo? Étienne has some shopping to do. He'll drop me off at the station.'

'Yes, fine.'

'It'll give the two of you some space.'

'Honestly, you're no trouble, Agnès.'

'I know. But we should all be playing with friends our own age. I'll go and wake him up. My train's at eleven.'

Étienne was curled up on the sofa with Éliette's cardigan thrown over his shoulders. Certain pre-Columbian mummies had adopted the same foetal position for their last journey.

'Étienne! … Étienne!'

Agnès's face appeared just at the point in his dream when he was finishing setting up a cycle race.

'What the fuck are you doing here?'

'I could ask you the same question. Why aren't you in your room?'

'I fell asleep in the garden. In the middle of the night I got cold and came and flopped down here.'

'I thought you were in with Éliette.'

'And what if I was?'

'Nothing. My train's at eleven. Éliette's lending us her wheels. I'm going to see my mate in La Ciotat. I'll be back tomorrow night.'

'What are you talking about?'

'The buyer I told you about last night. He's up for it, but he needs to try it.'

'And then what?'

'How should I know? We'll see what happens. So are you gonna let me do my thing, or what?'

'Yes. I think I might have a shower and get changed. You've got a face like a slapped arse.'

'I just want to get out of here.'

*

It was the first time the Aixam had left without her. Éliette watched the little cream car disappear at the end of the road and, for want of anything else to do, decided to sort out her paperwork. It felt strange to be alone in the house again. The 'strangeness' came from already missing him. Étienne had not been gone five minutes and she was already eagerly awaiting his return. Being alone felt different now. Less serene, perhaps, but how delicious it was to be filled with uncertainty: 'Is he coming back?' Waiting for someone, having someone waiting for you … No, nothing had happened besides their two hands pressed together between the sunloungers. Étienne had fallen asleep and she had left him in the care of the star-studded sky. It was important not to make any hasty moves. You didn't wake a sleepwalker standing on the edge of a roof. Agnès's departure this morning had not come as a surprise but seemed perfectly natural. She too must have felt that this Wednesday and Thursday were for them … only them. When she opened her eyes again, Éliette realised she had just torn her EDF bill into a thousand pieces of confetti.

Throughout the journey, Agnès had not stopped complaining about how fucking slow the piece of shit toy car was.

'I feel like I'm in a wheelchair. Put your foot down, damn it!'

'My foot's touching the floor!'

For the second time in Étienne's life, he found himself at Montélimar station. It was no worse than any other station, but he had no wish to hang around there. Agnès got out, slammed the door rather violently and went round to give her father a kiss through the open window.

'Don't do anything stupid, Étienne.'

'It's me who should be worried!'

'No. I'm going to do a deal: it's clear, straightforward; it's a certain amount per gram. As for you … you're putty in Éliette's hands.'

'What are you on about?'

'Watch out, Daddykins. The most dangerous thing about danger is that it comes where you least expect it.'

'Well, aren't you the philosopher.'

'I'm a wise old woman – older, even, than Éliette. I'll call you tonight.'

As she ran off into the station, bag slung over her shoulder, Étienne realised he had never seen her on the beach with a bucket and spade. One day they would go on holiday together. One day …

Éliette had given up poring over paperwork and gone back to the Colette biography. She read the first line of the fourth chapter for the tenth time, and still took nothing in. Nothing can fill the gap of waiting, other than a swift blow to the head. She had reached the point of wondering whether to cut her toenails or fingernails when the sound of an engine swept away all such noble thoughts. It wasn't the Aixam, but Paul's diesel engine. She let out a curse that was absorbed into the hush of the house.

'Hello, Paul!'

'Hi … Éliette. Gonna be a hot one.'

His speech was slurred, his step unsteady. His car was parked at an angle across the drive, its nose pointing into the ditch.

'Not disturbing you, am I?'

'Of course not. Fancy a coffee?'

'Not really the drink for this time of day, but if you like …'

'A pastis then?'

'I wouldn't say no.'

In the kitchen he instinctively sat at the table and took up the same position as he had the day before, elbows on the oilcloth, shoulders hunched.

'How's Rose?'

'All right. She's wilting.'

This unusual attempt at humour caught Éliette off guard.

'What about you?'

'Oh, just wonderful! One of my lads has just got himself killed and the other's about to marry a Kraut. May as well get the wedding and funeral done in one go!'

'You shouldn't be so hard on Serge. He's different, so what? He's hurting too. He loved his brother and he loves you.'

'Too much love, that's his problem! You can't go around loving everybody.'

'Why not?'

'Because … Oh, I don't know. Because it all becomes a mess, one big orgy! There are men and there are women, and it's complicated enough as it is!'

He downed his pastis in one, ran a hand across his face and looked at his palm as though trying to find his reflection in a mirror.

'You can't have it all, is all I'm saying!' he continued.

'Why? It's not a crime! Serge is gay and you've known that for years. He and his boyfriend love each other. Where's the harm in that?'

'Well, let me tell you, if I feel like doing ... with anyone I like, I ... It's a bloody joke! It's not right!'

Paul had stood up. He had gripped the edge of the sink with both hands and was tugging on it as if he wanted to rip it out. He was sweating heavily and his ears were as red as a tobacconist's shop sign. He looked to Éliette like a wild boar being chased.

'So you understand everything, do you? Everything's normal to you, is it? And what if I told you I've wanted you for years? What would you say to that, eh? What would you say?' he asked insistently.

He was now standing close behind her, his rough hands clamped around her shoulders.

'You're hurting me, Paul. It's the alcohol talking, and the pain you're in. You should go home.'

'I'm not pissed. I could drink a whole tank of pastis and I still wouldn't be drunk. Why shouldn't I get to do what I want, the way everyone else does? I want you! You have no idea how much I want you!'

Trapped in his gnarly arms, Éliette could do nothing but squirm in her chair, saying over and over again, 'That's enough, Paul. You're hurting me!'

But the harder she fought back, the tighter he gripped. His stubble scratched her cheek. Stale sweat and the taste of aniseed made her retch. They fell to the floor together. Paul's left hand clasped Éliette's face, while his right hand groped under her dress. His fingers were like tools, hard and coarse. His breath whooshed in her ear like a pressure hose. The more Éliette squirmed, the more Paul bore down on her, a ton of long-suppressed desire. He was on the verge of penetrating her when a noise rang out like a gong.

Paul let out a groan and fell onto his side, clutching his head. Étienne was standing above them with a cast-iron casserole dish in his hand.

'Don't just lie there, Éliette. Run.'

'Is he ...?'

'No, just stunned. Get out of here.'

Éliette limped out of the kitchen.

Étienne pulled up a chair and placed the casserole dish on his lap. Paul was moaning and wriggling on the ground like a big flaccid worm. Blood was trickling from his ear. He stammered, 'I didn't do anything! ... I didn't do anything!' Étienne kicked him in the side.

'Get out.'

Paul propped himself up on his elbow and stared at Étienne, red-eyed.

'Bastard!'

'Get out, before I do your face in.'

Paul got up on all fours and ran his hand across his blotchy face. He coughed, spat, and eventually got to his feet.

'You ain't seen the last of me ...'

'I'm telling you, fuck off or you're gonna get it!'

'This isn't over ... No way ...'

Paul glared at Étienne, his blue eyes washed out by pastis, and left, cackling like the witch in a bad dream.

Éliette had retreated to the living-room sofa where she lay huddled, clutching her knees to her chest. She wasn't crying but was shivering uncontrollably. Étienne sat in an armchair facing her. He was incredibly pale.

'It's OK. He's gone.'

Éliette could not unclench her teeth. Her heart was beating like a banging shutter.

'What can I do to help?'

Éliette raised her eyebrows, but couldn't produce a sound. She felt a wave of nausea rising in her stomach. She just made it to the toilet in time to throw up her breakfast. It took a good half-hour in the shower to scrub off the smell of Paul which had seeped into her skin. She got changed and threw her soiled clothes into the bin. Étienne was waiting in the garden, smoking a cigarette.

'Are you OK?'

'Yes, I think so. It's just ... unbelievable! Thirty years we've known each other ... I don't know what got into him ... I would never have imagined he was capable of ... I don't know what to do, Étienne. I just don't know ...'

'He was drunk. Maybe he'll apologise when he's sobered up.'

'Maybe. But I won't ever forget what's happened. Things can't go back to the way they were. What on earth's been going on the last two days? I don't have a clue any more! It's as if the whole world's gone mad, me included!'

'That's life, Éliette, that's all. You think you're safe, like when you're on the motorway; it's a bit boring, you lose concentration and then ... a loose bit of gravel, an insect, and whoops! You've lost control, spun round, and find yourself facing the wrong way. But hey, if you're not dead, you'll still end up somewhere! I bought some tomatoes and lamb chops. Do you fancy some food?'

'I'm not all that hungry.'

'Leave it to me, I'll sort it out. You have nothing to be afraid of now. I'm here, and I'm glad I am.'

He looked like a kid with his black eye and his cowlick, but Éliette felt safe with him. She took the hand he held out to her, and pressed it against her cheek. He smelt of fresh bread.

The microcar carried them along the winding, practically empty roads that criss-crossed the region for the whole afternoon. They dipped their feet in the emerald-green pools of the Escoutay and lay on the warm flat stones beside the river. From time to time a fluffy little cloud drifted across the sky above them and they would watch until it thinned and disappeared as if by magic. The babbling water mingled with birdsong like an advert for paradise, a bucolic, pastel-painted scene extolling the virtues of the afterlife. They stopped off in Alba where, after wandering down unevenly paved alleys that seemed to be populated only with cats, they enjoyed an ice-cold drink at a café under the plane trees in the square. A pair of pensioners were getting some air, sitting in their front garden. Side by side in their deckchairs, they didn't say a word to one another, looking straight ahead at a future that already belonged to the past.

'It's fascinating how still they are, isn't it? It's as if they've been there for ever.'

'They probably have. Look at their hands and feet – they're like roots!'

'It would be nice to live like a pot plant.'

'What's stopping you?'

'I don't know. I always feel like there's someone prodding me on, as if I'm shuffling along in a queue.'

'Why not leave the queue, Étienne?'

'I've tried, but I'm scared shitless of breaking ranks. Fact is I'm just an average Joe.'

The sun was beginning to yawn above the Roman-tiled rooftops. A handful of people had emerged out of nowhere and were crossing the square, a baguette under their arm, a shopping basket in their hand, everyday people, life's walk-on parts; Étienne would have liked to swap roles. He sighed and his eyes met Éliette's lavender-blue gaze. She was smiling.

'What?'

'Nothing. You're sweet when you're sad. Shall we go?'

In the car, they heard on the news that a twelve-year-old English girl had just given birth. The father was thirteen. When the child reached the age of twenty, it would have a thirty-two-year-old mother. Éliette remarked that, given we were all living longer, it would soon be hard to tell grandfather from grandson in family albums. But another news item, this time from the United States, suggested the opposite: two twelve-year-old kids had just been shot dead by police after gunning down half a dozen of their classmates along with their teacher. Christ dying at thirty-three seemed like a doddery old man in comparison.

They said no more to each other but sat thinking how quickly our time on earth is up, all the way back to Éliette's house. A crow was nailed to the gate by its wing, its head smashed in. Éliette hid her face in her hands while Étienne pulled the bird free and sent it on one last flight before it landed beyond the bushes.

'He's mad! My God, what am I going to do? I can't stay here any longer! I'm calling the police.'

'Calm down, Éliette. I'm here. I'm sure we can find a way to sort this out without making a song and dance about it. Trust me.'

Étienne put his arms around her and kissed her on the forehead. Trembling from head to toe, she clutched him tightly. Their lips met. She kissed like a little girl, mouth barely open, the shy tip of her tongue flavoured with diabolo menthe. As they closed the door behind them, Étienne told himself there was no rest in this world until you were six feet under a marble slab.

The telephone rang for the first time while Étienne was making a tomato salad. Éliette went to pick it up. It was Serge. His father had not been seen since that morning and Serge wondered if he might by any chance have been by. After a brief pause, Éliette responded in the negative, then asked after Rose. She was doing OK. The cousins from Aubenas were plying her with sleeping pills, leaving themselves free to sniff around in cupboards, suss out what the land and buildings were worth, and do sums on the backs of envelopes. There was such an atmosphere up there, he wasn't sure he could stick it out until the funeral. On that note, he wished her a good evening. He would probably pop in to say hello in the morning, just to be around some normal people.

Next it was Agnès's turn to call. She sounded completely hyper. Étienne could barely make sense of half of it.

'I can't understand a thing you're saying. Speak clearly!'

'I'm on a boat! It's awesome! Loads of people and champagne and stuff!'

'Good for you. What about the rest of it?'

'It's all good. I'll be back tomorrow morning. Ben's giving me a ride – and man, wait till you see his car! It's Italian, red, a proper racing car. Nothing like Éliette's little toy!'

'Are you out of your mind? You're not seriously planning on bringing this guy here?'

'Why not? He's got the dough, he's cool. No problemo, Daddy-o. We'll be able to get moving.'

'Agnès! Do not bring that man here. Do you hear me? It's not a block of hash you're selling, for fuck's sake. These people could stick a gun under our noses and skin us like rabbits. You're off your head. You need to drop it and get out of there, Agnès ... Agnès?'

'I can't hear you! ... This phone is a piece of shit ... Hello?'

'Agnès!'

'I'll call you back tomorrow. Oh, and don't do anything silly with Éliette. You know I'm the jealous type!'

'Agnès ...'

'Love you, you funny old fart.'

Étienne remained in conversation with the dial tone for a few seconds before hanging up.

They picked at their supper of tomato salad and a slice of ham. The bird nailed to the door had cast the shadow of its withered wing over the sunny afternoon. They opened a bottle of rosé and sat on the front step, sipping their wine and waiting for shooting stars to make a wish on. Éliette wished that Paul would fall into a hole so deep and dark he might never have existed. And she had two other, more minor, wishes: that Sylvie's children be bedridden with measles, and that Marc be forced to cancel his visit because of work (which would hardly be a surprise, after all). As for Étienne, he wished only to go back forty-five years and for a big fat star to hang permanently above his head. But all these comets, most of which were actually Russian or American satellites, were so laden with the petty hopes of humans in disarray that they left nothing but calling cards in the sky, along with the false promise that things would soon return to normal.

Since they could expect nothing from these tin-plated stars, Étienne and Éliette held one another close and waited for desire to make them climb the flight of stairs to Éliette's room. It was more of a big cuddle than a night of torrid passion. Both of them were tired, moving about in the bed as if in an aquarium filled with thick blue jelly. Having become used to Agnès's matchstick body – so easily set alight – he struggled to find his way around Éliette's, made timid and awkward by abstinence. But it didn't really matter: their fond strokes and caresses were enough to make them feel that one day they would have time, all the time in the world. They fell peacefully asleep, like two prisoners on death row clinging to the tiny hope of a presidential pardon.

In her dream, Éliette was doing the washing up, a huge great pile of it! She had barely finished one plate when someone handed her another. She could not tear her eyes from the foamy basin of clinking cutlery, glasses and saucers. She wanted to look up at the sky which she knew was so blue, but everything was going too quickly ... Still these anonymous hands were bringing piles and piles of dirty plates ... One of these went crashing to the floor, and she woke up.

'Étienne, I heard something!'

'Hmm?'

'I heard a noise. There's someone downstairs.'

'Stay here. I'll go.'

His dream had been filled with snow. Reach the summit and he would have won. But won what? ... He pulled on his trousers, wobbling in the dark, and left the room, coughing, his eyes still gummed up with sleep. It must have been around five in the morning; the pale light of dawn was creeping up the stairs like smoke. Outside, the birds were singing loudly, proud supporters of the breaking day. At the bottom of the stairs, Étienne hovered between the living room on his left and the kitchen on his right. He went for the kitchen, and the moment he stepped over the threshold, he knew what had been in store for the winner in his dream: a blow to the back of the head.

Pushing herself up on her elbows in bed, Éliette thought she heard a soft thud, like a pile of wet laundry being dumped on the floor, and then nothing.

'Étienne? ... ÉTIENNE?'

No answer. The light of dawn filtering through the slats in the shutters looked cold, like a grey shroud. She tried to cry out again but no sound escaped through the barrier of her gritted teeth. It was pointless. Someone was climbing the stairs, but it was not Étienne. Her fingers clutched the sheets while her eyes remained fastened on the half-open door, like an animal waiting for the butcher's axe to fall. We tell ourselves in books that we could jump out of the window, cry for help, lay our hands on a blunt object, do something. But it isn't true: fear paralyses you, makes an idiot out of you – the victim is suicidal, obediently waiting for the executioner to do his work. You know what's going to happen and you believe in it fervently, as though it were a form of deliverance. Perhaps it is all we have been waiting for, all our lives.

'Paul, why are you doing this?'

He had not yet pushed the door; only the barrel of his rifle pointed through the opening. He looked different, as though his profile had been etched on a bronze coin.

'Don't scream, Éliette. Don't scream or I'll kill you.'

The words were spoken calmly, as if to a restless child

at bedtime. His gun was in his right hand, and with the handkerchief in his left he wiped the sweat from his brow. He surveyed the room and, having established there was no riot squad hiding behind the wardrobe, he sat down at the foot of the bed. He looked like a hunter returning home empty-handed.

'I know it's not right, all of that … But all my life I've done the right thing and look where it's got me! I don't regret anything. I would have liked it to happen differently, but … all those feelings …'

He was beating his chest with the flat of his hand, and making the bed bounce. He had tears in his eyes, his gaze as clouded as his state of mind. Éliette let out a deep sigh. Perhaps there was a way out after all.

'Why don't you put down your gun?'

'I can't … If you scream, I'll shoot you, obviously.'

'Why?'

'Because that's just the way it is! … You spend your whole life trying to find a place there's no way back from. That's where I am.'

'What have you done to Étienne?'

'That stupid little bastard? He's not dead; I just gave him a good whack round the head. He's tied up downstairs. What the hell do you see in that idiot, anyway?'

'He's a friend, Paul. Just a friend!'

Paul was now standing again, the barrel of his gun chasing the shadows.

'He's no man, Éliette! No man at all. He'll hurt you, I'm telling you. I know what men are like – I was in Algeria!

Up in the Aurès mountains, you soon sorted the men from the boys. I stood and watched the prisoners dig their own graves ... *Bang! Bang!* ... *He* is not a man, believe me.'

'You're scaring me. Put the gun down.'

He looked at her, dazed by his own rant, and began smiling as if he knew her game.

'I may not be the sharpest tool in the box, but I'm no fool, Éliette!'

'What do you want?'

'I don't know any more ... Good, evil, it's all the same ... Smashing that little bastard's head in was fun, just like nailing that crow to your door ... Doing wrong ... that's it, that's what I like.'

'You won't get anywhere with that attitude.'

'Who cares? I'm already there! I'm not afraid of anything any more! Anything at all!'

He banged his head against the door several times to demonstrate how pain made him numb. A trickle of blood ran down from his bandage, skirting his nose, to the corner of his mouth. He stuck out his tongue and licked it.

'It's nice. Tastes a bit like rust. I'm rusty, Éliette, just like you, just like everyone. We're all dead, only no one else knows it yet.'

Éliette shifted her weight on the bed. Paul stiffened.

'Don't move!'

'I need a wee.'

'Piss in the bed! Yeah, that's right, piss in front of me. I'd like that ... Go on then!'

Using the tip of his rifle, he pulled back the sheets, exposing Éliette's bare abdomen.

'Well? Is it coming?'

'I can't ...'

'You'd do it for him, though, wouldn't you, slut? But not for me ... Well, from now on you're going to do all that filthy stuff in front of me. Even if I drop dead, you'll always have me there with you, in your dirty shitty little memories! No one's going to forget me!'

The barrel of the gun brushed against Éliette's nose. She could smell its acidic metal odour. Paul's eyes bored into hers, incandescent with rage. She didn't even have the strength to faint. Paul lowered his eyes first. The two black holes, set one on top of the other in the barrel of the gun, turned towards the window ledge, where a blackbird had just landed with much flapping of its wings. Paul let the weapon fall into his lap and burst into tears.

'Forgive me, Éliette. I'm not a bad person ... but what am I supposed to do with all the bad stuff that's happened? I want another life too! Do you think I chose to be a bloody yokel? To go to bed with bloody Rose every night? Of course I didn't! I've dreamed of going places, just like everyone else. I've just never been lucky enough to live my dreams. Maybe they've turned to nightmares now, but they're still my dreams, they're mine! It's all up to me! Damn, yes!'

Éliette was holding her breath. One false move and Paul could go up like a powder keg. In spite of her terror, she could not help feeling a little sorry for him. He was right:

a nightmare was a dream that had gone wrong. Her bladder was straining. It was silly, but she was sure that if she could only go to the loo, everything would be better. Paul would calm down, everything would fall back into place, just like it was ...

'Do you remember when the kids used to play together? All laughing and shouting! Hmm? Do you remember, Éliette?'

'Yes, Paul. I remember.'

'We were happy back then. None of us could have imagined that one day ... Know what I think?'

'No, I don't, but I really need the toilet ...'

'Your friend, downstairs – I think it was him who killed my Patrick.'

'Why would he have done that? They didn't even know each other!'

'I don't know. But I'm sure it was him. Ever since he's been here, everything's changed. You're not the same, Éliette, nothing's the same. It's not just a coincidence!'

'Let me go to the loo and then we can talk about all this calmly ...'

Paul wasn't listening. He rubbed the trigger of his gun as if stroking a clitoris.

'I'll get rid of him. We've got to tackle him, like mildew.'

'Paul, please ...'

'Huh? Oh, all right, but I'm coming with you. You have to leave the door open. I can't trust you. It's not your fault; he's pulled the wool over your eyes, but I'm here. I respect you, Éliette. You can count on me.'

She got out of bed, naked, and Paul coyly averted his eyes while she put on her dressing gown. As she relieved herself, with Paul standing guard outside the door, the rifle over his shoulder, she could not help finding a modicum of truth in Paul's ramblings. Of course, he was raving mad, but there was no denying that since Étienne had appeared, everything had turned upside down. The abandoned car that had caused Patrick's death, Étienne strolling down the road, the way he had acted in front of the gendarmes, the story he had told about the girlfriend leaving him in the middle of nowhere, and Agnès, whose behaviour towards her father was so unlike what one would expect of a daughter ... There was nothing concrete or certain any more, as there had been in Charles's day; even the tiled floor of the bathroom seemed as treacherous as shifting sand.

'Done?'

'Yes.'

Paul had red eyes. He looked like one of those briar pipe bowls carved in the form of a sailor's head.

'Don't you think we could do with a nice cup of coffee?'

It may have been the sound of the flush upstairs, a waterfall in his dreams of mountains, that woke Étienne up, or perhaps it was the shooting pain behind his ear. It was only when he tried to lift a hand to his head that he realised he was tied up, his wrists and ankles so tightly bound he could feel them puffing up like rubber gloves filled with water. A filthy hanky had been shoved in his mouth. Inside his throbbing head, his thoughts were jostling together and pouring out like a bag of marbles in a schoolyard. With his cheek pressed to the red floor tiles, he could see the undersides of the dining chairs with their battered straw seats and the table pocked with woodworm, along with a tiny mouse with round eyes, creeping the length of the skirting boards like a wind-up toy. He made an attempt to sit up, but the rope binding his limbs also went round his throat, preventing him from making any movement on pain of strangulation. He heard the door open and saw Éliette's bare feet (one of which had the beginnings of a bunion forming) rushing towards him, followed by Paul's heavy boots.

'What on earth have you done to him? Étienne, are you all right?'

The question struck him as somewhat absurd. He made do with rolling his eyes and grimacing.

'Paul, you're not going to …'

'Just make some coffee, Éliette. Don't worry about that …'

Éliette and Étienne exchanged a look punctuated with ellipses as Paul sat down heavily, mopping his brow.

'Gonna be a hot one today. Storm's on its way back in. No good this weather, coming and going; nature can't get its bearings.'

He sat with his rifle between his knees as if newly returned from a hunt, a good honest man full of concern for his land and ready and willing to discharge his weapon at the slightest move by Étienne. Éliette's hands were no longer hers; they moved of their own accord, putting coffee in the pot, rinsing two cups, taking the sugar out of the cupboard – they could easily have done without her. Éliette was working on autopilot. She didn't dare cast her eyes towards Étienne – taken the wrong way, a single glance could prove fatal to both of them. The sound of the birds chirruping outside made the situation all the more surreal. If Étienne had not been lying on the floor, it was just like countless other mornings when Paul had come round and she had made him coffee.

'Two sugars, yes, thanks, Éliette … Oh, I don't think I told you: the other night we were in Clément's car coming back from Privas and we hit a wild boar – eighty kilos, the thing was. We cut it up the same night and chucked the head and the skin down the old well – you know, behind the old rubbish dump. Quite handy that well – all you have to do is throw a few bits of scrap on top and the gendarmes are none the wiser! Bet people have got rid of some interesting stuff down there …'

As he said this, Paul turned to Étienne.

'Rose and I thought you might like a haunch to have with your kids. We put one in the freezer for you.'

'That's very kind of you, Paul, but if you want us to stay friends you need to untie Étienne and put your gun down.'

'You're having a laugh! You saw him whack me around the head with your pan! Four stitches I had to have!'

'Yes, but remember what you were doing to me!'

'I was drunk, Éliette. It doesn't count! And anyway, you

94

know very well that's not the only thing. He's the one who sent Patrick into the ravine, no shadow of a doubt! Don't try to fool me you've known him ten years!'

Once again, doubts began rising in Éliette's heart like a corpse surfacing from a bog. Étienne's wide eyes pleaded with her.

'Let him explain himself, or let's call the police. You can't just go round accusing people without any proof!'

'Aha! You see – you've clicked something's not right, too! I'm telling you, I know what men are like. You didn't call the police out in Algeria. You made them dig their hole and job done! Next!'

'But we're not at war any more, Paul, and even when we were, that wasn't …'

'Of course we're still at war! Thugs like him are roaming the streets. The towns are full of them and they're crawling all over the place here too, ruining things for everyone!'

'But for heaven's sake, Paul, what do you think you can do about it?'

'Some housekeeping! But not the kind women do. He knows exactly what I'm talking about. Isn't that right?'

The barrel of the gun lifted Étienne's chin; his face was pale.

'Paul, I know you're hurting, but this whole thing is ridiculous. I'm calling the police.'

'No, Éliette. These things are best sorted out man to man. Don't do anything stupid. Besides, I've cut the phone lines.'

'You what?'

'You're not on my side, Éliette. He's turned you. I don't want you to be angry but I just can't trust you. I'm going to have to shut you in the cellar while I finish the job. You'll thank me later.'

The sound of a car pulling up outside made Paul leap up and point his gun at Éliette.

'No funny business, OK? Or this is going to get nasty.'

There were footsteps on the gravel and then a knock came at the door. Serge's voice called: 'Éliette? … Papa?'

The oak door creaked open and soon Serge and Zep stepped into the kitchen, dressed in shorts and white T-shirts.

'Papa? … What the hell are you doing with that gun? … We've been looking for you since …' (Éliette discreetly drew his attention to Étienne curled up on the floor.) 'What the hell's going on here? … Papa?'

'This has nothing to do with you! What's going on here does not involve queers!'

'You're insane!'

'Tell your Kraut not to move or I'll blow his skull to pieces.'

'Papa, please, put down the gun!'

'Think you can tell me what to do, you little shit? On your knees! Everyone, on your knees! Even you, Éliette. Hands on your heads!'

Serge took a step forward. Zep moved away to the left, while Éliette pulled a chair in front of her. Paul stepped back.

'Fuck. The first person to make another move gets it!'

It was like a game of grandmother's footsteps. Everyone froze.

'Papa …'

'Shut up! You're all against me. I'm the only one who knows! That fucker there killed your brother but you don't give a shit! None of you do, because you never loved him, because Patrick was twice the person any of you will ever be!'

'Stop it, Papa! Let Éliette's friend go. We'll say nothing about this – it stays between us. If you won't untie him, I will. I loved Patrick just as much as you did.'

'Like hell you did!'

'I did, for fuck's sake! Even if I've known for years he wasn't yours!'

'Shut your mouth, Serge! Don't you ever say that again!'

'This has gone far enough! Let this man go. You're not the only one having a hard time. Have you forgotten Maman, back at home?'

'Your mother's a slag!'

'And Clément's your good friend – but what does it matter now? Look, I don't blame you for anything. Are you going to untie him or shall I?'

'Take one step and I'll kill you.'

'You know, Papa, I don't care if you don't love me, I still love you. Please, put the gun down …'

'Who told you? About your mother and Clément?'

'Everyone knows. Please, this is ridi—'

Serge didn't have a chance to finish his sentence. A sort of scarlet explosion speckled the wall in fragments of bone, brain and blood. The second shot hit Zep with full force, passing through his chest like a cannonball. The bang echoed around the kitchen for several seconds. Outside, not a bird was singing. They had all fled towards a boundless sky where human folly dissolved into wispy clouds that were munched like candyfloss between big blue teeth.

Éliette's ears seemed to be stuffed with cotton wool, and her lower jaw was practically touching her chest. Her eyes could not take in what they had seen and could still see now: the bodies of the two young men immobilised in grotesque poses, an arm here, a leg there, pouring with black blood that branched out into a complicated network of streams running between the floor tiles. Serge's right hand rested on Étienne's face; making short muffled cries as he moved his head from side to side, Étienne struggled to shake it off. There were unidentifiable splatters across his hair and forehead. Soon the stench of excrement mingled with that of gunpowder.

Paul let go of his gun and fell to his knees. His trembling lips muttered words that could not be made out. Éliette rushed to the sink and threw up the two coffees she had just swallowed. When she lifted her head two minutes later, Paul had not changed position. He was intoning words as though reciting a psalm, something along the lines of 'That's it, now, we're there …' Étienne had finally managed to wriggle free of Serge's corpse and was resting his head against the wall. His throat was swollen – he was choking, the handkerchief sticking out of his mouth like a fat purple tongue, eyes rolled back. A ray of sunlight bounced off a kitchen knife on the draining board. Éliette slowly took hold of it, but as she did so, Paul let out a hoarse shout and did something incomprehensible. He undid his right shoe, took it off, yanked off his sock and took the rifle in his hand. Éliette was clutching the knife tightly against her chest when he turned towards her.

'There's no need, Éliette. We're there, we're there.'

He thrust the barrel into his mouth and used his big toe to pull the trigger.

The minute Éliette had cut Étienne loose he had run into the bathroom with one thing on his mind: to strip off his soiled clothes and wash and wash and wash some more, from head to foot. But as the water ran and the soap lathered up, the bathtub filled with ever pinker liquid. Blood produced blood until the house was nothing but one huge open wound that seemed never to want to heal. He had brushed his teeth several times and still could not get rid of the indelible taste of rust and grease that the dirty hanky had left in his mouth. He needed to jet-wash his entire insides, his memory, his heart, wished he could watch it all disappearing down the plughole. Afterwards, Éliette helped him rinse the white enamel and the tiles. Étienne stared into the mirror, scrutinising his reflection in microscopic detail; every time he ran his hand through his hair, he was sure he could feel scraps of bone and brain under his nails.

'Jesus fucking Christ! I'm never going to get it out!'

'There's nothing left, Étienne. It's all gone.'

'No, it hasn't! Look, here! … And here! It's still there!'

It took a very long time for Éliette to convince him to see reason. He could not bring himself to move away from the mirror; all the muscles in his body were so tight they could snap. As she draped her dressing gown over his shoulders, she felt as if she was dressing a wooden mannequin. She led him across the kitchen like a blind man, helping him to avoid the pools of blood and the bodies strewn here and there, with bluebottles already hovering above them. When they reached the sitting room she sat him on the sofa and poured him a shot which he downed through gritted teeth. And then, sitting with his head hanging, he told her everything: about the train, the coke, stealing the car, Patrick's accident, everything, except his relationship with Agnès.

He was sobbing now, his head still down. She had rarely felt so calm, so collected in all her life. Her hand stroked the lump at the nape of his neck; he could have confessed to the most sickening crimes and still she would not for one second have wavered in her love for him. It was a strange kind of love, both maternal and carnal, innocent and perverted, and it made her incredibly happy. For a few seconds, Charles's face came to her. He was smiling at her from the afterlife the way he smiled when she owned up to a minor sin, and he would shrug and open the paper, whose headlines were full of catastrophes and massacres from one end of the earth to the other.

'Étienne, you ought to go and get dressed and hide this briefcase of yours. Bury it under the compost heap. I'm going to have to go to the police station. You needn't worry about anything. Étienne, can you hear me?'

Étienne stood up. With his puffy eye, the lump on his neck and the too-tight dressing gown, he looked like a boxer approaching retirement.

'Yes, good plan. I feel better. I was so afraid it was going to be the end of me … How on earth did he know it was me? His son, I mean …'

'Instinct. He was a good huntsman. A good father, too. Will you be all right?'

'I think so.'

'I'm off then. Everything's going to be just fine – you'll see.'

'Éliette! … Why?'

'I love you, and that's all you need to know.'

'But what do I …?'

'I'm asking nothing of you.'

Étienne made no reply. With all his body and soul he wished he could love like she did. He heard the unmistakable sound of the Aixam fading into the distance and went upstairs to change.

He had only black, grey and beige clothing. None of it suited him.

The sound of another car reached his ears as he was pulling on his trousers, a high-power engine, out of place on this dirt track. Through the bedroom window he saw Agnès step out of the Ferrari, laughing, with a thickset guy – not very young, not very tall, not very attractive – following her. When she saw him, she waved up at him. Tangled in his trousers, he didn't have a chance to shout, 'No! Don't come in!'

'Come in, Ben, let's have a coffee …'

Agnès froze as she opened the kitchen door. Étienne had

come hurtling down the stairs, and Benito was peering over Agnès's shoulder at the scene before him.

'Madonna!'

Étienne barged in front of them and tried to bar their way. Agnès stared at him, so pale she was almost transparent. She could not utter a single word. The Italian's eyebrows were practically touching the roots of his hair. He stepped backwards until he reached the front door, where he turned and ran. They heard quick footsteps on the gravel, the roar of the engine starting up again, and a screech of tyres. Agnès and Étienne stared hard at one another, as if meeting for the first time. Their gazes joined to form a bridge over the unspeakable. The multiple horsepower of the Ferrari gave way to the flies buzzing over the bodies. Open-mouthed and wide-eyed, Agnès looked like a Pompeii fresco.

'It wasn't me, Agnès! It wasn't me!'

Her sunglasses had fallen on the floor. Étienne trod on them; it was like walking on his daughter's eyes.

'I'm telling you, it wasn't me! Go up to your room and get undressed. You were asleep, you heard gunshots, that's it. Quick, the cops are on their way. I'll explain later. Run! I have to go and stash the case. Go!'

Agnès stared at him uncomprehendingly, as if trying to find a use for an unfamiliar tool. He had to push her up the stairs. The police van arrived a few minutes after he had buried the briefcase under the compost heap.

For the entire morning, the house was invaded by flies and police. More and more of both kept arriving. There were people taking photos, measuring things, scouring every corner. It sounded like a swarm of bees was nearby: no individual noise, only a worrying murmur. In the garden, in the shade of the summer dining room, an inspector whose slight squint made him always seem to be talking to someone else was taking statements from Éliette, Étienne and Agnès.

Éliette had not batted an eyelid when Agnès appeared dressed in the men's shirt she wore to bed. All three claimed to have spent the night at the house. In the morning, Éliette and Étienne had heard a noise in the kitchen. They came downstairs and found Paul in a state of extreme agitation. He threatened to shoot them. When Paul's son and his friend arrived, there had been a brief altercation over a family quarrel, and Paul had fired on them before turning the gun on himself. No, they didn't know why he had cut the phone lines, or how he had come by his head injury. Clearly he was aware of Serge's intention to visit Éliette, and he had ambushed him. This moment of madness could be put down to the pain of the loss of his son.

The three bodies were carried out by the men in white and shoved into the back of an ambulance which drove off, its wheels narrowly avoiding the ditch. It was like any of the countless petty stories that made it onto the front page of the local paper before being turned into fish-and-chip wrapping. The inspector with the wandering eye put his notepad away and sighed.

'Gonna be another hot one today. Right then, we'll need you to stick around in case we require anything else from you, but it all seems tragically straightforward to me.'

'Inspector, we can't stay here ... It's ...'

'I understand, Madame. For the time being, nothing is to be touched. A cleaning company will be along when we finish. In the meantime, go and stay with friends or check into a hotel, somewhere we can get hold of you if need be.'

'In that case, we'll be at the Relais de l'Empereur in Montélimar.'

'Ah yes, I know it well. The food's excellent!'

'Well, you know ...'

'Of course, sorry. We'll be in touch with you there.'

'Would you be able to call us a taxi on your phone? Only my ... car can only carry two people.'

'Oh, the little Aixam! My dad's got one ... Yes, but I could give one of you a lift. Want to hop in, Monsieur?'

Étienne bit the inside of his cheek.

'That would be great, thanks.'

Two gendarmes remained at the scene. Éliette and Agnès saw Étienne disappear inside the inspector's car, holding himself upright, almost rigid.

'Air con all right for you back there?'

'Yes, fine.'

Étienne was suffocating in the back. The river they were

driving alongside was nothing but a trickle of green water snaking between white pebbles, draining away.

'Always makes you feel guilty, sitting in a police car, doesn't it?'

'Not me, no. I'm just ...'

'Of course, of course, sorry. I forgot myself. So what's the story with that black eye and the bump on the back of your head?'

'There isn't one. It was an accident. I fell off a ladder.'

'Just what you needed! You're not having much luck at the moment, are you?'

'Apparently not.'

'No, apparently not.'

They didn't exchange another word until they reached the hotel, where the inspector dropped him off and told him not to worry about anything.

In the microcar, Agnès and Éliette had barely more to say to one another.

'This car is a pile of crap.'

'It's a pile of crap.'

'How are we going to get anywhere in this?'

'We'll get as far as the Relais de l'Empereur.'

'And then what? Some adventure this is going to be.'

'Don't you think your father's had enough adventures recently?'

'Think he's ripe for retirement like you, do you?'

'Ripe for a bit of peace and quiet, I'd say.'

'I don't like you.'

'I don't hate you either.'

'You're making him old.'
'He wasn't expecting to meet me.'
'I was.'
They said nothing more.

As in all the places where Napoleon had left a strand of hair, the Relais de l'Empereur was decorated with golden bees, wall hangings and furniture of uncertain age, and peopled with staff so practised at bending and scraping that an avant-garde choreographer would have applauded them. Agnès smirked when offered a room adjoining that of 'her parents'.

'That'll be handy in case I have a nightmare, won't it, Papa?'

'You should go and have a shower. We'll meet back down here in half an hour.'

Éliette was already showering in her room. Agnès was starting to get on her nerves, along with all the other children in the world. What exactly did they have against their parents? What made them want to spoil what little future they had left? There was Agnès with her double-edged remarks; Patrick, who had, in a sense, caused his father's end and his mother's breakdown; even Serge and his provocative love life; even Sylvie, even Marc, who took her for an imbecile, as if she was incapable of leading her own life! Why couldn't they just leave their parents alone? Why were they still getting under their feet, just as they had when they were in nappies? She wouldn't be surprised if the younger members of society couldn't even pay towards their elders' pensions. Sick and tired of this unscrupulous generation that let the grass grow over the living corpses of their fathers and mothers.

There had been big scientific advances and it was now possible to live to a hundred. It was an old person's world – they had made it after all, and if it didn't suit the young, they could make one of their own. Marc and Sylvie were so far removed from her universe that it had not even crossed her mind to contact them. She had stopped being a mother in order to take a second chance at being a woman, barely living in the present moment. They no longer belonged with her. She would call them later. Recent events had provided an excellent excuse to put them off visiting. Afterwards, she would set things straight with Agnès. There was no way she was going to pass on the opportunity of the new life opening up to her like a long-awaited past. She returned to the bedroom with a towel wrapped around her hair.

'Étienne, I'm going to put the house on the market.'

'I understand.'

'Would you ... would you like to live with me?'

Étienne propped himself up on his elbow and blinked madly.

'Excuse me?'

'I'm not asking you to love me, just to be with me. I know there's something between us – I don't know what it is, but it's enough. You're at your wits' end; you can lean on me. We could be happy together, living in peace.'

'Éliette! We've known each other a matter of days and I've brought you nothing but trouble.'

'Exactly. That needs to change. You can't carry on living like this. Admit you're tempted?'

'I am, but it's impossible. There's the case, there's Agnès ...'

'Forget all that! You have a right to be happy!'

'I'd love to, honestly, Éliette, but I can't. I have to see this through.'

'Through to what? Prison? Death? Do you think that's what Agnès wants? I've a bit put away. If you want we can leave tomorrow. We can give Agnès some money. She's young ...'

'Éliette, please ... I need to think. My head hurts.'

It was true. His brain was being jolted inside his skull like the clapper in a bell. Agnès, Éliette, *ding-dong*! Left to his own devices, he probably would have gone to the police station and told the bog-eyed inspector everything just to get it over with. The slightest thought unleashed a wave of pain inside him, spreading from the tips of his toes to the top of his head.

'Knock, knock. Can I come in? ... Blimey, why the long faces? Trouble in paradise?'

Éliette shrugged and disappeared into the bathroom. Agnès stifled a giggle.

'Wipe your nose – it's covered in coke.'

'Oh, sorry! Right, well, I've got the munchies. See you downstairs.'

Three o'clock in the afternoon. Montélimar was booming like a burst drum. A dreary pizzeria provided a place to sit, stale pizza and dry pasta. At the end of this dismal meal washed down with vinegary wine, Étienne, as if playing the tourist, had the absurd idea of asking what there was to see in the town. After several moments scratching his head with its shiny black mop, the sad Mickey Mouse-faced waiter suggested the Château des Adhémar. He had never been there himself, despite being a native of the town, but had heard it was worth a look. The view from up there was supposed to be amazing.

It was a painful slog up to these ruins, which had been spruced up by generous donors. The sun was not even out; it was just muggy. Agnès moaned at every step, like a child being dragged around beauty spots during the summer holidays.

'Where are you taking us? ... These alleys stink of dog shit ... My feet hurt ... I need to pee ... I've got indigestion.'

All three were suffering from heartburn, but they still made it to the foot of a pile of yellow stones. Your twenty-franc fee bought access to the castle's sad, empty keep and a few metres of rampart.

'Amazing view? Yeah, right! I get a better view every morning washing my arse. It's an utter hole!'

'Agnès!'

'What? Am I wrong? The whole town's like a cemetery. It's like a model someone forgot to finish.'

Below the fortifications, an old woman bent like the arch of the castle's portal was walking a dog whose hind legs were mounted on wheels.

'Let's get out of here, Étienne. There can't be many places worse than this.'

The wind had picked up. It blew under the Roman roof

tiles, playing a monotonous chant as irritating as the songs of the Peruvian bands at Châtelet métro station. They would have liked to shoo it away.

'Come on. Let's go before you end up looking like that mutt.'

'I think your father's capable of making his own decisions.'

'Fuck off! He's not your lapdog.'

Leaving … it was all Étienne had done, his entire life. He envied the stone – or molasse, as it was known here – crumbling where it stood. Swallows punctuated the space between passing clouds like commas. A bell was ringing somewhere in the sky. Éliette leant out to listen.

'A wedding …?'

Closer to the edge, Agnès replied, 'No, a funeral. Screw this, I'm off.'

She left them leaning out over the parapet. They watched as the red of her hair bounded down the dark alleyways like a glowing fag end.

Back at the hotel, Éliette called her children. Their voices sounded unreal, like those of air hostesses. Without going into detail, she informed them of the deaths of Paul and Serge. Given the circumstances, they probably shouldn't come. This was actually for the best all round because, as expected, Justine's measles had passed on to her brother; as for Marc, a meeting had come up which he couldn't get out of, and he would have had to cancel anyway. Although, if she wanted to come and stay with either of them … No, she would rather rest, perhaps even go and stay with friends near Marseille, clear her head, she didn't know, it was all so … She would let them know. They were thinking of her, of course, and she of them. These things happened. Speak soon.

As she hung up the phone, she felt a great weight lift off her. She had bought herself some time. It might only have been worth a few coins in a begging bowl, but at least it was something, like a cigarette and a glass of rum.

Étienne was sleeping, or pretending to sleep with an arm over his face and his legs crossed. While he was at her house, part of the furniture like an insect trapped in cut resin, anything was possible. But now, in the middle of this boundless freedom, she wasn't so sure. She felt like a young bride on her wedding night. She hardly recognised this man who had shut himself away in a semblance of sleep. Through the wall, a fuzzy noise was coming from Agnès's TV.

'Étienne, are you asleep?'

'No.'

'What are you going to do?'

'I don't know. I'm happy here, now.'

'Let's leave, Étienne. We'll go wherever you want, Morocco ...'

'I was inside for a year there, there's no way I want to go back. Why are the pair of you so fixated on making me leave?'

'It's not the same with your daughter.'

'Listen, Éliette. I abandoned my daughter when she was a year old. I owe her. I can't have done all of this for nothing! I want to do something good for once in my life, for her. You can't imagine what it's like to have never had a chance in life. I want to give her that. And then, yes, we can do whatever you want. I like you a lot, Éliette, I really do.'

'Well then, leave those filthy drugs with her and let's be happy! You'll not want for anything, you—'

The telephone rang. The inspector's voice on the line was as disconcerting as his cross-eyed gaze, but he had only good news to impart: everything had been put back in its proper place at her home and the case would soon be closed. There was no doubt over what had happened: a moment of madness that had ended in tragedy, and which they would do their best to keep out of the local papers. A cleaning company would be sent in to sort everything out the next morning, and her phone line would be reconnected as soon as possible.

Speaking of which, had she by any chance thought of any reason why Monsieur Jaubert had cut the line? … No, never mind. Ah, one other thing: they had found a rope and a pair of blood-soaked trousers in the dustbin, ring any bells? … No. Not to worry, they could talk about all that when they came to sign their statements the next morning. A formality. With that, he wished her a good evening and advised her to try the Relais de l'Empereur's excellent *côte de bœuf*.

Éliette could not decide whether to tell Étienne about the inspector's discovery. It was silly of them not to have told the truth, but when they had discussed doing so before she went to the police station, Étienne had been categorically against it. They would have asked why Paul had singled him out, and he was anxious to avoid having the spotlight turned on him, given his past. How could they have been so stupid? He had reacted as if he was guilty of something, out of habit, no doubt. By doing his best to stay out of it, he had achieved the exact opposite. Tomorrow, the police would be bound to find this omission suspicious.

'So?'

'Everything's fine.'

'It doesn't look fine.'

'It is. But they found your trousers and the rope in the bin.'

'Shit!'

'We'll have to tell the truth when we go tomorrow. Just tell them you were in shock. You haven't done anything wrong – you saved me from being raped!'

'You don't know what they're like. Anyone who's done time is guilty in their eyes. I can see him coming at me with his wonky eye, asking "Why this?" and "Why that?" What if they find my fingerprints on the car? That fucker's sniffed me out like a dog. I'll get five years, at least!'

'You're behaving like a child. Trust me, for goodness' sake! It can't go on like this. You're innocent. You saved me!'

'I don't want to go back there, Éliette. I can't face it!'

'Then you have to do as I say, darling. Enough of all this, enough of being scared!'

Étienne lit a cigarette. It tasted like dust.

'But what about the briefcase? … And Agnès?'

'I'll talk to her. I'll see to everything. You have a rest.'

'No, I should tell her. But yes, I agree with everything else. Let's do that.'

When Étienne had closed the door behind him, Éliette let her head fall back on the pillows, a faint smile on her lips. Cronus was devouring his children.

*

The section of McDonald's drinking straw and the razor blade lay across one another on the still powdery surface of the pocket mirror. Agnès ran her finger over it and rubbed the remnants into her gums. There was almost nothing left of what she had taken with her to the coast. The local anaesthetic did not produce the desired effect. It would have had to reach her heart for that, a heart as crumpled as Éliette's neck.

She grabbed the remote and cut off the dull stream of local news.

'What the fuck am I even doing here?'

Without admitting it to herself, she had spent almost the past two hours listening out for noises from the adjoining room. She had heard murmuring, then a phone ringing, and then nothing. It was the silence that was driving her mad. They were fucking, she was sure they were fucking. At that age, you didn't cry out or moan; you did it on the quiet, so Death didn't hear you.

'Idiot! I'm such a fucking idiot!'

Agnès had never been able to lay into anyone but herself. It was handy always to have your victim within arm's reach. She must have got this from her father. Him, in there! ... The years had kept them apart, and now a miserable wall of brick and plaster stood between them. The old slag had won, with her wrinkles, her stupid little car, her horrible house and a future built on bus passes. It was quite funny when you thought about it. The pair of them could snuff it under a heap of cross-stitched cushions for all she cared! Let him suffocate while he pounded away at her ancient, hairless pussy.

She, on the other hand, had her whole life ahead of her,

though it hardly looked like a happily ever after! She would fetch the damned case and get as far away from her shitty past as she possibly could. Her mother had died of an overdose when she was thirteen, and these days her father could barely keep his head above water. So let him die, let him suffer! Life had cheated her from the word go, made her think she'd be left with only the crumbs. Oh, no! She was going to gorge on it, and feed her leftovers to everyone at her feet. Bastard! Piece of shit! Father, why have you forsaken me? …

She spat out the nail of her right index finger at the same time as her 'yes' in reply to the tentative knocks at her door. Étienne's face looked like a mop that had not been wrung out properly.

'All right?'

'Better than you, by the looks of it.'

'We're going down for dinner.'

'I'm not hungry. Unless they have snails. I can't eat anything but snails.'

'Agnès … We've got a bit of a problem with the police. They found … Anyway, the point is, it's nothing to do with you. Tomorrow Éliette's going to give you some money and—'

'And I'll get married and have lots of children. Are you taking the piss? What about the briefcase?'

'We'd do best to forget about it. We can build new lives for ourselves.'

'Sure, crummy little lives, while two kilos of perfectly good coke sits under the compost heap … Do you think I'm a fucking idiot?'

'I swear I'll help you! We need to put an end to all this.'

'You're not exactly a walking advert for sex with the elderly. It's made you soft in the head. So you're trying to ditch me again?'

'Agnès …!'

'She's got you wrapped around her little finger, the old slapper! You've fucked around long enough, and now you want to leave me out in the cold! Well, you can't! Think about what you're going to get from her. A wheelchair and a little handjob at Christmas. You deserve better, Daddy dear, and so do I! I'll take your fucking case and cart it around with me wherever I go, cross borders with it, no problem. I'll take it to China if I have to! I won't let you leave me twice, you old bastard. We're joined together, you and me. Joined!'

'What are you suggesting?'

'We keep a low profile. You play along and keep your mouth shut. Later on, I'll go and get the case. We meet at the station. You buy two tickets to Rome – I know people there; the addresses are in my bag. Éliette will go back to being Éliette, and we … we'll carry on being what we are. You can't turn me down. You can't do anything except love me.'

'Do me a line.'

In a glass globe, everything is back to front. The snow always falls the right way.

'What? You haven't got snails?'

'No, Mademoiselle.'

'Even tinned ones?'

'Certainly not! Everything's freshly made here.'

'Fine, I'll have an ice cream then.'

'For your starter?'

'An ice cream, I don't care what flavour but with Chantilly cream – and lots of it!'

'Very good, Mademoiselle.'

There were very few people in the hotel dining room, but those who overheard Agnès's order held their forks in mid-air. Éliette and Étienne hid behind their menus.

'What? I can order an ice cream if I want, can't I?'

'Don't you think you might be overdoing it a bit?'

'No, I don't, Daddykins. All I want is an ice cream and to get out of this hole as soon as possible. Don't you want that too, Éliette?'

'You read my mind. And you didn't even need to ask your mirror on the wall.'

'Oh but I did ask. Mirror, mirror ... Mirrors covered in snow ... Whatever. The pair of you can do what you like, but I'm getting out of here, OK? I'm moving on. Éliette, if you'll take me back to fetch the case, I'll disappear. How does that sound?'

'What about your statement to the police tomorrow?'

'You can write me a sick note.'

Under the table, Éliette's hands were strangling her napkin. Étienne seemed unusually interested in the ceiling mouldings.

'Fine. Let's go straight away.'

'Great! I'll go and get my bag. Bye bye, Daddykins, and don't worry, I'm kosher. As soon as the deal's done, you'll be getting your hands on your pension.'

The two women rose, as did the eyebrows of their fellow diners. When the waiter brought over a sorbet dripping with Chantilly and two vegetable terrines, there was no one left at the table.

'What's this factory?'

The Aixam's headlights swept over the towers of Cruas nuclear power station.

'A nuclear plant.'

'Why have they painted a naked kid playing with water on it?'

'Probably to make us all think the atom is perfectly safe.'

'It's dumb. Kids aren't afraid of atoms; they're all over the place.'

'What are they afraid of then? The big, bad wolf?'

'No. Their parents.'

The road slithered snake-like through the countryside. All they could see was blue or black, as if these were the only two colours left on earth. The journey seemed to go on for ever, the little car making painfully slow progress. Agnès never stopped crossing and uncrossing her legs, nervously drumming her fingers on the dashboard.

At last the house appeared at the end of the track. It looked like an abandoned dog. Éliette barely recognised it. In the space of a few hours, the haven of peace she had pampered like a pet all her life had become 'the murder house' that people would drive past quickly, crossing themselves, before it became derelict because nobody wanted to buy it. Despite the reassuringly thick walls, misfortune had found its way in and laid its cursed eggs. She could not live here any more. For a split second, Éliette had a vision, blurred by the tears welling in her eyes, of Charles with his chest bared, mixing cement, and then of Sylvie and Marc spraying one another with the hose, and it all disappeared for ever when she cut the headlights.

'What's wrong?'

'Oh, nothing. I've just turned a page, that's all. Be quick. Go and find your filthy stuff and I'll drop you at the station. I never want to see you again.'

'No danger of that!'

Agnès got out of the car and disappeared into the porch. Éliette had lost her home, her memories, but she had gained Étienne. When he had returned to their room earlier, having seen reason, her heart had leapt in her chest. She was sure it would work out fine with the police. It was the memory of his prison days that had made him lose his head. He had stopped Paul from assaulting her. They would understand. It was all just an unfortunate combination of circumstances. Of course nothing would ever be the same again, but there were still so many pages of life to get through. Charles would have given her his blessing. As for Agnès's departure, taking the briefcase with her, she couldn't have wished for more. Oh, she didn't despise the poor girl, but truth be told she didn't give a damn what became of her. Sometimes, only selfishness can save you, even the good Lord knows that, He who condemns suicide.

Agnès reappeared, briefcase in hand.

'You haven't got a cloth, have you? This thing stinks! You country people are unbelievable. You want to grow flowers so you let a pile of crap sit rotting right under your windows!'

'That's exactly why the flowers smell good. Here's a cloth.'

Agnès rubbed it over the case, cursing filthy nature for being full of dead creatures, poison mushrooms, stinging nettles and insects that bite.

'Hey! Look at that! … A dead crow!'

Éliette jumped at the sight of the bird Paul had nailed to the door.

'Leave that! Let's go.'

The lights on the dashboard made it feel like they were inside an aquarium. They could have been at the bottom of a lake, were it not for the Aixam's throaty cough.

'Agnès?'

'Yes.'

'If you love your father, I think it would be best if you didn't see him again for a little while.'

'If I love my father? … And what if he loved me?'

'Of course he loves you, the same way any father loves his child …'

'The same way? Or … some other way?'

'What are you getting at?'

'Oh, poor Éliette! We've moved on from the days of steam engines. Know what we were doing when he came to my room earlier? … He was fucking me, and we were going for it like you've never gone for it in your life!'

'Agnès!'

'And not for the first time either! … Two months it's been going on. Well, that's shut you up, hasn't it, love? It's not our fault, you know; we didn't find out we were father and daughter till it was too late. Life's a bitch like that, isn't it? But at the end of the day, if we love each other, who's to judge us? Don't worry – we're not planning on having kids together.'

'You're lying. You're just saying it because …'

'Because it's true, just like the fact he's waiting for me at the station so we can fuck off together, somewhere, anywhere, who gives a shit.'

'I don't believe you!'

'You don't want to believe it, but it's the truth! 'Cos I've got something you ain't. So you've got your house and your little car, and you smile away like a happy little garden gnome, but I make him hard. HARD!'

The entire night sky burst out laughing in Éliette's face; the universe had creased up, the trees were in stitches, the river beneath them giggling between the rocks, and for good reason! Watching from his cloud, Charles himself was doubled up with laughter, slapping his thighs as the little car kept dead ahead while the road bent round.

'For Christ's sake, what the fuck are you doing?'

Just in time, Agnès grabbed the steering wheel and slammed her foot on the brake. The Aixam swerved, grazed one tree and came to a standstill against the trunk of another. The night sky had fallen silent. A red-faced moon tried to hide its shame behind the clouds.

'Jesus! You could have killed us! Éliette …?'

She was slumped over the steering wheel, her shoulders shaking. Agnès rubbed her elbow.

'Can't even kill yourself properly in this stupid fucking car.'

She got out. The ground swayed beneath her feet and she fell onto the grass. Never before had the silence seemed so full, an amalgam of thousands of tiny sounds: a falling leaf, a crawling insect, a passing breeze, a breaking bud, the water bubbling away below … It amounted to almost nothing, with darkness all around, but she was alive. Then came the sound of the car door slamming and the sight of Éliette, as she opened her eyes; Éliette lifting a rock above her head, a rock as big as the moon.

Montélimar station, unlike that of Perpignan, is less the beating heart of the city and more its back end. In a shady corner of the concourse, Étienne was beginning to regret not having sided with Éliette. A tramp with a mangy dog and a nasty stench had just squeezed ten francs and a cigarette out of him. The effect of the two lines of coke he had done in Agnès's bedroom had given way to a frightening sense of disarray. Inside his head was an incredibly complex maze which he weaved through frantically like a lab rat. The state he was in was not wholly down to what he had taken. Having spent three-quarters of his life high, until prison brought him down again, Étienne knew exactly what to expect from a hit. No, more worrying than drugs was the unbelievable addiction to life that paradoxically kept pushing him to get into deeper and deeper shit. His record was hard to top. He had become a kind of world champion of failure, a haggard wayfarer of the road of relationships. Éliette? … Agnès? … Queen of hearts? … Queen of clubs? … Though he knew it was stupid to dither at life's crossroads since the road taken must always be the right one, the others having become mere figments of the imagination, still he could not make up his mind. Escaping, anywhere, but on his own, seemed the wisest option. So what if some called that cowardice. No one but him was in his shoes …

He stood up, threw his bag over his shoulder and began to laugh to himself, like a kid playing a prank. He was going to disappear, simple as that, walk through the night, and all the next day, and so on like the fool in a tarot set. He had barely stepped out of the station when the little Aixam pulled up in front of him.

'Éliette!'

'Get in … Don't just stand there, get in!'

He obeyed, open-mouthed like any village idiot. The microcar's right eye wandered like the inspector's, and the wing was crumpled. No sooner had he taken his seat than Éliette put her foot down.

'What's happened? Have you had an accident?'

'Nothing serious. Agnès is dead.'

'What are you talking about? Are you mad?'

'Maybe!'

'Where are we going? This isn't the way to the hotel … Tell me what's going on!'

'We're driving. It's seven minutes past eleven, and we're driving south.'

'I don't know what's gone on, but you're making a big mistake, Éliette.'

'No. I've done that already.'

Éliette's profile seemed to be carved in stone; she didn't so much as blink. She stared straight at the road ahead of her, oblivious to the honking of horns as she was repeatedly overtaken.

'Something's catching on the front right-hand wheel.'

'Yes, it is.'

As they drove out of town, the road sign with MONTÉLIMAR struck out looked like a funeral wreath with a red ribbon pinned across it.

'Why don't we stop and you can tell me all about it?'

'No. You've been doing your best to go nowhere all your life. Well, now you can.'

The sound of something rattling in the back made Étienne look over his shoulder. The handle of the briefcase was bumping against the window.

'You picked up the case?'

'When you're going nowhere, you have to take your baggage with you.'

'For fuck's sake, come on! Stop messing around. Where's Agnès?'

'Hey! Stop shouting! Agnès is nowhere, just like you, just like me, just like everyone.'

'Fine, be like that. You'll have to stop eventually to get petrol.'

Étienne reached for the handle of his door. The Aixam wasn't exactly speeding along, but it was going fast enough for a fall onto the tarmac to be fatal.

'What about our date with the law tomorrow?'

'They won't miss us.'

'No, of course not! This is ridiculous. You said yourself everything would work itself out.'

'I was wrong. I've killed your daughter, don't you get it? … Bashed her head in with a rock. It's just the two of us now.'

'You're not serious.'

'All the bridges are burnt now. The past is gone; now everything's in the headlights ahead of us …'

'I don't believe it. I don't believe it!'

'Me neither. I used to believe, but I don't any more.'

'But why? Why, damn it?'

'You're asking me why … Please. Take a holiday; stop acting like a bastard. It doesn't suit you.'

The lab rat in the maze suddenly came to a halt. The note of sincerity in Éliette's voice was crushing any vague hope of escape. If there had been a way into the labyrinth, there was surely no way out. It was pointless fighting it; all he could do was wait, and thank the heavens for the reprieve that had come in the shape of the Aixam's engine gasping for breath. The for and against had finally joined hands, slotting together like the pieces of a jigsaw whose picture you guessed long before it was finished. Going from one tragedy to the next, you eventually reached a nebulous nirvana, ending up more or less back where you started.

'You killed Agnès …'

'Yes. She told me about you two. I could have understood, but I was so hurt … You should have told me.'

'I couldn't even admit it to myself.'

'You know, it's not the incest that shocked me so much as the way you played me for a fool, or rather the way you played at life without me. I love you, Étienne – I would have understood; I could have been your ally. You needn't have been afraid of me. It's the fear of fear that did for us. I didn't hate her, you know; I could have accepted it. You don't try to compete when you're my age. If you like, I'll drop you at the next service station.'

Étienne's heart was like an Agen prune: shrivelled and black. Darkness was closing its fist around the ridiculous little beige car that no outlaw in his right mind would have used to make his getaway. In spite of everything, the kilometres of road kept coming, like parts of a never-ending telescope. They passed through villages with peculiar names. Chairs were being put away on café terraces, and soon the only light came from the street lamps looming over them like the eyes of a dinosaur. What they felt was more akin to the sensation of teetering on the edge of a vertical drop than of chasing the horizon. They shared the silence like a cell, without hope of escape.

As they rounded a wide bend in a sort of shadowy creek, the blinking pink and blue neon lights of a truckers' café, or a nightclub, or something, made Éliette slow down.

'I'm thirsty. Let's stop.'

'OK.'

A dozen cars were parked outside, each sporting a white tulle bow. The puffed-out Aixam nestled in among them. The air was pulsing to the binary rhythm pumping out of the building. As soon as they stepped inside, they were confronted with a thundering rendition of 'Macarena'. A hundred or so people were writhing about on the dance floor, dripping with sweat and screaming along to the chorus. Waiters weaved their way through the crowd, hair slicked to their foreheads, carrying trays laden with glasses and bottles. Here and there children slipped under the tables and popped up to down the dregs of drinks. Just like in photos of family celebrations, everyone had red eyes – only here it was not the fault of the camera. The tang of sparkling Clairette de Die hung in the air. Éliette and Étienne gradually manoeuvred their way to the bar. Cupping his hands around his mouth, Étienne asked the glassy-eyed barman for a Coke and a beer which they drank while pinned to the wall. The bride – for a wedding was the cause of this bonanza of animal magnetism – was a tall, skinny brunette. A fine layer of bluish fuzz covered her upper lip, suggesting the rest of her body might be equally hirsute. Wearing the Barbie-doll outfit of her dreams, she swung on the arms of her guests, twisting her ankles on her high heels, a permanent smile slapped on her horsey face. As for the groom, he could have been any one of the prematurely aged, bleary-eyed young men singing at the tops of their voices, ties loosened, blue suits bursting at the seams, never to be worn again. The oldest and ugliest members of the party sat, deafened, eyelids heavy, around the edge of the room, their chins resting on ample chests or distended stomachs. A dishevelled-looking girl moving with difficulty in a tight lamé dress tried to make Étienne join a wild farandole around the room. Her sticky hand slipped between his fingers like a fat fish. There was no need to pay for anything. No one had fingers left to count on, or clear enough vision to keep an eye on things. In a few rare circumstances, the little people play rich. It takes them the rest of their lives to shake off the horrendous hangover, if not longer!

Neither the Coke nor the beer had quenched their thirst. But the fine spray from the night sky was now spitting in their faces. As he was about to get back into the Aixam, Étienne noticed that the keys to the car parked next to theirs had been left in the ignition. The car, which no doubt belonged to the wedding couple, was more laden with flowers than a hearse.

'Éliette, wait!'

'What?'

'Get the case and the bags out.'

'Why?'

'Just do it!'

The luggage was transferred from one vehicle to the other. Étienne got behind the wheel while Éliette sat in the passenger seat. An incredible racket like the sound of bins being emptied followed their departure. Étienne pulled over a hundred metres down the road to detach all the saucepans and chamber pots that had been tied to the bumper.

'We're not going nowhere any more; we're going everywhere.'

The tulle- and flower-adorned Citroën XM waited for a greengrocer's van to give way before rearing up and galloping into what remained of the night.

The speed, the real speed of a real car thrilled Étienne and made Éliette's legs stiffen plank-like in the footwell. The trucks and cars they overtook seemed to be treading water. Éliette stared goggle-eyed at the night's gaping mouth, as they steamed towards it. The heady scent of the bouquets heaped up on the back seats was getting to her.

'All these flowers are making me feel sick.'

'Open your window and chuck them out. It stinks of cheap happiness.'

The wind rushing at her head stopped her breath. One by one the sprays of roses were scattered on the tarmac in a firework display of multicoloured petals.

'Better?'

'Yes.'

'It's got the fire of God in it, this motor!'

'As if the devil were biting at its heels. We'll get there quicker in this car.'

'I don't want to go anywhere any more. At this rate we'll be at the Italian border by daybreak.'

'And then?'

'We'll be Italian. This wedding car is worth all the passports in the world. They'll let us through in this, no question. No one will say a word. We're on honeymoon! Rome, Naples, here we come!'

Éliette burst out laughing despite herself. It was stronger than she was; she had just realised that for her entire life she had been two people and that the other Éliette who had played second fiddle for so long to the sweet version of herself – the good wife and mother, the dignified widow – had just taken charge. And she was capable of anything. With her head tipped back and a strange smile playing on her lips, she gave in to sleep. Étienne put the radio on. Bashung was singing '*Ma petite entreprise* …'

A milky cloud was beginning to lighten the sky when Étienne pulled over. His eyes were prickly and his stiff jaws could no longer hold back the yawns. Éliette was still asleep. Soundlessly, he slipped out of the car. The dawn was thick with birdsong, as if this was the very first day on earth. He lay down with his arms spread wide, facing the horizon that rolled on as far as the eye could see. The sky was blushing like a girl's cheeks after a profession of love. The XM's bonnet was boiling hot. Through the windscreen, Éliette was dozing calmly, her head resting on her shoulder. For all Étienne repeated to himself that this lovely, gentle, peaceable lady had just killed his daughter, his mistress, by smashing her over the head with a rock, he could not bring himself to consider her guilty of anything. She was innocent, just like him, like the worst criminal, like the dog who kills the cat, the cat who kills the mouse, the mouse who … must kill something too. All around, in the bushes and the grass, prey and predators mingled in the same macabre dance. You could be one or the other, depending on the circumstances, all of which were extenuating. It was what they called life, the strongest of all excuses.

By way of breakfast, he took a sniff of coke off the point of the knife. Éliette opened her eyes at the same time as a streak of white powder shot across his brow.

'Where are we?'

'About sixty kilometres from Ventimiglia. How are you feeling?'

'Too early to say. What are you doing?'

'I took a sniff to wake myself up. Want some?'

'Why not?'

Étienne took a bit from the bag.

'You have to cover one nostril and breathe in very hard with the other.'

'You don't think—'

'Forget what you've read in the papers. If it wasn't good, no one would take it.'

Right nostril, left nostril, Éliette closed her eyes and slumped back in her seat. She expected to sink into a universe out of a Hieronymus Bosch painting, teeming with horned monsters and grimacing gargoyles, but instead of seeing infernal hallucinations, she found herself breathing fresh mountain air. It was like opening the window on the first day of springtime.

'Well?'

'It didn't do anything for me ... or maybe it did. I have the impression of being incredibly normal.'

'There you go, that's it.'

'I need to pee.'

The grass bounced beneath her feet like the fluffiest of carpets. Squatting behind a bush, she watched the sun rising above the patchwork of fields as if seeing the spectacle for the very first time. It was as if she had been myopic her entire life; never before had she seen so clearly and precisely. They ought to make bread with this strange flour, to give humanity its sight back. It made you wonder why the stuff was illegal. She was not unsteady on her feet, wasn't tripping over her words like a drunk, on the contrary! She had never been more alert in her life.

'Étienne, I'm hungry.'

'Me too.'

The little village they stopped in resembled a giant pot of geraniums. The flowers were bursting from every window sill, carpeting roundabouts, growing in between the bricks of the houses.

The light mist from the fountains made little rainbows form against the blue sky. Everything seemed clean and fresh, like a soft-boiled egg with its top cut off. The yellow yolk of the morning sun ran down the roads. The beribboned XM could not have parked against a better backdrop. The waiter in the nearest café greeted them with a flourish.

'My first customers of the day! And a pair of newlyweds to boot! I'll look after you. Sit back and make yourselves comfy!'

The nightmare was giving way to a dream. Everything that was happening seemed so totally natural and crystal clear that neither Éliette nor Étienne batted an eyelid. Life was regaining the upper hand because it was at home here. They ate a hearty breakfast of eggs and ham for Étienne and warm croissants with jam for Éliette. From the café terrace, they watched the growing crowd of people out walking with baskets on their arms and poodles on leads, everyone polished, gleaming, almost metallic, as if they had all just left the same hair salon. The air smelt like something you could bottle.

'You know, Éliette, we should give ourselves a makeover. Newlyweds should have a bit of sparkle about them.'

The waiter gave them the coffees on the house – starting the day's business with newlyweds (even wrinkly ones) must bring luck!

Éliette bought herself a striped T-shirt dress that looked like a sailor's outfit, while Étienne picked up a pair of white jeans. They rounded off their purchases with a pair of sunglasses each and even a basket which they filled with a bottle of champagne and a jar of caviar, to really complete the newlywed look. The Italian customs officers welcomed them with open arms as if they had been waiting for them all their lives. It was such a relief that they took the risk of doing another little line in the car park next to the customs post. The sun showered them with laughter that no night could ever extinguish. Every Italian had a mandolin in his throat. They stopped in the first hotel they came to, with an ochre front and palm trees in the garden. There, as the daylight beat its drum against the shutters, they made love as if defying gravity.

It was very mild and the roads were filled with people casually strolling and taking the air, breathing in the blue pigment of the night sky. Étienne and Éliette were sitting on the terrace of a little restaurant overlooking the sea. By the glow of paper lanterns, they were tucking into a *fritto misto* accompanied by a bottle of Lacryma Christi. It was as lovely and as idiotic as a scene in a *fotonovela*. Yet Étienne seemed to have something on his mind. He looked like a sergeant major putting the finishing touches to a plan of attack.

'I think it would be safest to ditch the car tomorrow. We can take the train to Rome. Agnès left some addresses in her bag. I shouldn't have too much trouble shifting the case.'

'We'll keep a bit, though, won't we?'

'Éliette! … Yes, a bit. And then—'

The remainder of his sentence was carried away by the insect-like buzzing of a Vespa. Not that it mattered much; Éliette agreed to everything. She smiled as she sipped her drink, giving herself up entirely to this new-found happiness she had never dared imagine possible. She felt immortal, miraculously cured, even if she knew perfectly well that her state of mind was largely due to drugs. They had taken more in the bedroom before heading out for dinner. And so what, where was the harm in it? Forty years of yoga to achieve nirvana or a split second's inhalation, the result was the same. The hunger, this bulimic urge to live, justified the means.

'Why are you laughing?'

'If one of my children had told me last week that they were on drugs, I'd have been worried out of my mind.'

'Just be a bit careful. It's not a magic bullet. It comes at a price.'

'I think I've paid in advance. I've been retired; I deserve my final showdown. What do you think of this ashtray?'

'The ashtray? It's just like any other ashtray. Why do you ask?'

'I want to take it as a souvenir.'

'I'm going to ask for the bill. I'm tired.'

Étienne settled up, but as they left the restaurant they were stopped by the waiter.

'Excuse me, but please could the lady give back the ashtray she put in her bag?'

Étienne went green. He babbled muddled excuses until Éliette handed back the stolen goods.

Back on the road, he began almost running. The looks of passers-by seemed hostile; the Vespas were conspiring to run him over. The devil had set foot in paradise.

'Étienne, what's come over you? … Wait!'

'You're out of your mind! Do you think now is the time to get ourselves noticed?'

'Oh please, there's no need to fuss! It must happen all the time. All right, sorry.'

Étienne didn't feel at ease until he had locked the door of their hotel room behind them. Lying on the bed with his eyes glued to the ceiling, he only unclenched his jaw to take a drag of his cigarette.

'Étienne, this is ridiculous! Everyone does silly things every once in a while.'

'You're not everyone! … Draw the curtain please.'

Éliette reluctantly did as she was asked. The night sky was so beautiful, like the one Van Gogh painted while wearing candles on his hat. She was sincerely sorry; how fragile their dream seemed to be.

'Will you forgive me, please? I'm going to order a bottle of champagne – do you want some?'

They were brought not champagne but Asti Spumante. Not that it really mattered; it was the lightness of the bubbles they needed. After two glasses and another line each, Étienne had reconciled himself to life, but a knot remained in his chest like a wrecking ball. They talked, both making extravagant plans and recalling fragments of fictitious or muddled memories. This blend of equally hypothetical pasts and futures was a kind of lifebelt that kept them afloat amid the treacherous waters of the present. Around four in the morning, exhausted, having run out of words, they let the night pull black wool over their eyes. Étienne woke with a start two hours later, his mouth apparently lined with blotting paper. In his dream, Agnès had been shaking something in her hand, something like a salad spinner. She was shouting, 'It's ready, Papa, it's ready!' It was a severed head, with blood spurting from the sawn neck onto virgin snow. In the fog, he could not see whose head it was.

He got up and went to drink as much water from the tap as he could manage. It was warm, and tasted of toothpaste. He splashed his face. Outside, daylight had come, a pearly white sky like an oyster, the sun struggling to break through the clouds. A breeze lifted the curtain like a veil, but otherwise everything hung flat: the clothes on the backs of the chairs, the fake crystal chandelier, the seaweed-floppy terry towels, his cheeks, his arms, his balls. It was going to be muggy today.

Éliette groaned and rolled over as he lay back down next to her.

'Is it morning? What time is it?'

'Six thirty.'

'Can't you sleep, my love?'

'Yes, yes, I was just thirsty.'

'Is it nice out?'

'Grey.'

'Come here … closer …'

She felt for Étienne's body under the sheet. She found his thigh, the pelvic bone jutting out, his hand, his shoulder, but it was like stroking a statue. Not a shiver, not the slightest quivering muscle.

'Is something wrong, darling?'

'No, no, go back to sleep.'

She snuggled against his shoulder, murmuring something like, 'Everything's fine, everything's fine.' Étienne ran his hand through his hair as his gaze followed the grey light creeping in through the folds of the curtain like a toxic gas, and went back to sleep thinking to himself that the end of the world was not a big black hole, nor a multicoloured firework display, but, all the more stupidly, it was a day like any other, only a little overcast.

They left the hotel around ten o'clock, Étienne having barely touched his breakfast. He could not have said exactly what was wrong. He felt like the sky: a bit low. Despite her best efforts, Éliette could not instil her good mood in him, and this upset her.

'Won't you tell me what the matter is?'

'I don't know. I had strange dreams. It's left a weird taste in my mouth. It's this car; I'll feel better once we've got rid of it.'

They headed out of town on a coastal road. Étienne drove slowly as if seeking a picnic spot, looking out for tracks either side of the road where he could abandon the car, but found none suitable. Éliette was baffled. As far as she was concerned, any old parking space would have done the job, but Étienne pressed on, determined to find 'the right place'.

'Étienne, it doesn't matter. We're wasting time.'

'No, I know what I'm doing. We need to put it in a place where no one will find it for several days.'

'All right, fine.'

As they drove out of a village a kilometre or so further on, Étienne leapt out of his seat, pointing a finger skywards.

'There! That's the place – do you see it?'

A flight of gulls was circling in the air above a sort of truncated volcano with white gases rising up from its summit.

'Is it a landfill site?'

'Yes! That's the spot. It's as if I knew where I was going!'

'There might be people there.'

'No, we'll push the car in from up there. It'll soon be covered by tons of rubbish. It's perfect!'

Éliette remained unconvinced but, at the end of the day, whether it was here or somewhere else ... She just wanted him to stop obsessing about this and move on. They turned down a small bumpy track that ran through a pine forest. The further they went, the stronger the acrid stench of burnt rubbish became. They eventually came into a clearing that looked down over the landfill site. It was deserted but for the gulls scouring the rubbish, pecking here and there and letting out piercing squawks. Étienne seemed as happy as a little boy who has won a treasure hunt.

'It's brilliant, isn't it?'

'It smells horrible.'

'Let's take it up to the edge. You get out with the bags and all I'll have to do is give it a little shove. It's nice here, isn't it?'

'Uh ... There's a certain charm to it, but I don't know that I'd spend my holidays here.'

Étienne rolled slowly forward. With every turn of the wheels, worrying cracking noises could be heard – crates, cans, piles of boxes. A fridge wobbled in front of them, its door hanging wide open. Withered plastic bags flew up like sluggish hot-air balloons. The birds stirred up the air, which was thick with the stench of rotten cabbage. Étienne appeared fascinated, peering over the steering wheel. Soon there was nothing ahead but the void waiting to swallow them.

'Étienne! Don't go any further, we're right on the edge!'

'Huh? ... Oh, yes.'

The car came to a stop. Shielding her eyes to avoid looking down, Éliette got out, her legs trembling. Her feet sank into a pile of warm filth. Étienne was still clutching the wheel, dazzled by the emptiness before him.

'Étienne! ... Étienne!'

'Yes?'

'I'm getting the bags out. Let's push the car off and get out of here. It's making me dizzy.'

He had the same smile on his face as on the day she had met him by the little bridge, and the sight of it lifted her spirits. Wading through the nauseating sludge, she took out the bags and the briefcase and moved back a few metres. Étienne opened his door, took off the hand brake and turned towards her with his hands in the air, beaming.

'We did it!'

He leant against the car and it started to wobble. As it began to tip, a gust of wind slammed the door closed, trapping Étienne's jacket. It happened before Éliette could even cry out. She heard the sound of crumpling metal as the car fell apart thirty metres below, and the thwack of the gulls' wings as they scattered, screeching off into the white sky. And then nothing but tumbling rubbish.

She stayed still for a moment, as if dazzled by a camera flash, before falling to her knees, her head in her hands. In the darkness between her palms she saw Étienne's face as he realised the trap had closed on him, his mouth opening to utter a word he would never speak, and his hands flailing in thin air. Click, clack!

She had no tears left, only spasms that shook her back. She stood up and with all her might threw Étienne's bag to the ends of the earth, where she now found herself. She opened the briefcase, tipping out the contents of one of the plastic bags which puffed out like a white cloud on the wind. She was about to move on to the next bag when she saw the gulls returning one by one, perching on broken mattresses and bicycle wheels. They were watching her with their beady little eyes and ruffling their feathers as if to say, 'No need to make a song and dance about it. If you're not dead, you must be alive.'

Éliette closed the briefcase, turned her back on the sky and began walking down the bumpy track.